The Book of Tara

MARICLAIRE NORTON

Copyright © 2022 by Mariclaire Norton

ISBN: Paperback 978-1-958856-02-4
eBook 978-1-958856-03-1

All rights reserved. No part of this publication may be reproduced, distributed, or transmitted in any form or by any electronic or mechanical means, without the prior written permission of the publisher, except in the case of brief quotations embodied in critical reviews and certain other noncommercial uses permitted by copyright law.

Printed in the United States of America

Dedicated to my most wonderful husband and muse and the Alaric to my Tara.

Chapter One

THE LIBRARY WAS OLD and dusty. It looked like no one had been in it for decades, maybe even centuries. Maeve sighed. It would take years to make any sort of sense out of the place, she knew. But she only had to find one thing: the lost Book of ArdRighian Tara of Eirlandia. Although the ArdRighian and her consort, King Alaric, were only the stuff of legends now to the general public, Maeve knew that they had actually lived. If she could find the book, and safely return it to Kilawey, then she could help bring peace back to this land.

The old legend stated that if the rightful ArdRighian of Eirlandia should, of her own free will, marry the King of the Vikes, then peace would come for all time to the two lands. Of course, as with all legends, this feat was easier said than done as the new couple had to first have the respective crowns of the original Tara and Alaric, the legendary rulers of Eirlandia and Vikland who brought peace between their peoples all those centuries ago.

As a Fighdrui, Maeve knew more than the average Eirlandian regarding the true history of her country. Steeped in the Old Magic and with knowledge of High Eirl, the language used by the Drui spellworkers, Maeve had an advantage over even the scholars. It was widely believed that the Book of Tara revealed the location of the crowns, hidden away centuries ago, just before their deaths. All she had to do was find the Book. She hoped that once she had returned to Kilawey that Aelfund, the head of her order, would allow her to lead the expedition to retrieve the crowns as a reward for her work here.

"Okay," Maeve muttered to herself, "time to find the sealed vault." She shifted the tote on her back, and turned on the all-light. The dark interior was suddenly illuminated brightly. Smiling grimly, she left the all-light there and started forward. She would use her smaller lights once she got beyond the main room. She needed the interior completely lit, however, so she could read the signs that pointed to the various vaults that led off from the main chamber.

A member of the scholarly class that was also trained in fighting, Maeve had no fear of anything being in this place. Although she was only of average height, her weight was almost all muscle. Besides magical knowledge, she was well trained in the combat arts, both defensive and offensive. Her gray-green eyes were sharp sighted, and though she had a pixie look about her, she had been told she was as hard as granite and as strong willed as iron.

Maeve's clothing, to an outsider, would proclaim her status as a Fighdrui. Dressed in dark green trews and shirt, her belt held many pouches with various tools and even healing potions. Her cloak, now discarded and at her campsite, was the distictive blue and green stripe of the Fighdrui. She had left her horse at a small waystation over a day's travel away, but she knew it would be well cared for by the keepers. The abandoned, ancient library was close to that part of Eirlandia held by the Rebel Righs, and she had had to move on foot in order to bypass their scouts. Trained in tracking as well as her other skills, Maeve had disguised her passage and had arrived in early morning to her destination. This would, she had reckoned, give her plenty of time to find the Book of Tara and leave a different way without incident.

Maeve knew that nothing lived in the Library, which had been magically sealed and which she had had to open upon arrival. That said, assuming she found the Book, if word got out before she made it back Kilawey, then she might have to fight her way to the capital.

It saddened Maeve that her country was in the midst of civil war. Many of the lesser Righs had rebelled against the current ArdRighian Tara's rule, claiming they would not follow a woman. Some of these rebels, it was said, were even in contact with the Vikes, asking for help to depose the ArdRighian. So far, Vikland had refused to interfere, and that was due mainly to their king, Alaric, who many in their country felt was the reincarnation of the original King Alaric, the consort of the original ArdRighian Tara.

Beyond the rebel Righs, there were also many warlords and tribal kings who would not want the crowns found and returned to Kilawey. These men, while technically neutral, provided soldiers and weapons to both sides of the war. They would stand to lose great profits should peace ever happen between the Eirlandians and the Vikes.

She ventured forward, remembering the words the ArdDrui had spoken to her before leaving Kilawey. "The Great Library was destroyed just after the deaths of Tara and Alaric," Elaroth had told Mauve. "The ArdDrui of the time, Cullucan, sealed the vault and concealed its location so that the warring factions could not find the book. When the rebel armies invaded the library; just after their battle with the royal armies, but before Cullucan had been able to seal the entrance; they knew the book was hidden somewhere, but they could not locate the chamber. They took out their frustration out on the rest of the building. Many important works were lost because of their anger and destruction."

"The rebel Righs did not find the vault because it was hidden in plain sight," the ArdDrui had continued, "but in a place they would not think to look. Each new ArdDrui is told the location of the vault at their investiture, but only a Fighdrui is allowed to actually find and return the book. That was another surety that Cullucan placed so that the book would not fall into the wrong hands. Be careful, be cautious, but you should come to no harm in that place; at least not from the place itself. Follow my instructions and look for the vault's opening where the book stands open for all to read, yet the page cannot be moved."

Maeve wandered through the many stacks of books and overturned shelves, climbing over the piles when she could not go around, sorry for every footfall that caused even more destruction to the Pagi beneath her, but there was nothing she could do about it. Once the crowns were found and peace returned, then the scholars of Eirlandia and Vikland would both come here to begin the work of preserving and restoring what they could. Until then, the words of the past would have to survive as they could.

About halfway down the main aisle, Maeve noticed a sigil placed on the floor. To one not trained in High Eirl, it would have been seen only as a decoration. But the design was much more than that; it indicated a direction for a searcher to go to find the book.

"Down this way lies the path to the past," the sigil read. *"Do not let appearances deceive, for while all may gaze, only few can read."*

Maeve smiled slightly; she now had a clue of where to go. Taking a smaller all-light, she proceeded down the smaller aisle that led off from the main corridor. Sweeping the light left and right, she shortly came to what appeared to be the end of the passageway. A small alcove appeared in front of her, with a statue of a large book, opened to a page sitting square in the middle. The words in the book were written in High Eirl so, like the sigil before, would have been unreadable to only a few even at the time of its installation and even fewer in this time.

Following the instructions on the book, Maeve spoke the words which would give her entrance into the vault. Slowly the massive book moved, and a small doorway appeared where it had been solid wall. Taking the light with her, Maeve moved slowly into the hole, unsure of what she would find.

The corridor was not long, and Maeve soon found herself in a small but well-appointed chamber. A few tables and chairs were strewn about, and there were even old all-lights lining the walls. More importantly, however, was the large display case in the center of the room. Walking closer, Maeve realized the material was almonite, a rare mineral that was used to protect extremely fragile and precious objects. Being almost impossible to break, and also being extremely costly, almonite was used only by the ruling class and only on very rare occasions. It was a mineral that took magic well, so the only way to create an enclosure of this size would have been to use magic in its construction. That alone told Maeve she had found what she sought.

Coming closer, Maeve saw that other objects had once rested with the book, and she wondered what they might have been. Only the book remained, however, and Maeve knew she was the only one who had laid eyes on this treasure in centuries.

There was no latch to this case, but Meve knew it would have been sealed with magic. Maeve had already been provided with the opening spell, so she knew opening the case would prove easy. Maeve sighed and ran her finger through her short red hair. Having found the book, she became aware of how dusty she felt. Her tan, form-fitting tunic and leggings were several shades lighter than normal because of the dust in the library. She would need a bath once she was done. "Okay, Lass," she thought to herself. "First things first, let's get that book."

Before she did anything else, however, Maeve spoke the words to turn on the old all-lights that dotted the chamber walls. The lights turned on dimly at first, but soon grew to a good glow. The light would make it easier to do some preliminary checking of the book. Turning off her small all-light, she put down her pack on a desk and approached the book.

The Book of Tara was not large. Since it had been the personal journal of the high ArdRighian, it was of an easy size to handle. The cover was made of a leather-like substance, although Maeve was sure it was something stronger than hide, for it showed no signs of age or disintegration. Using her hands to create the appropriate pattern, she spoke the opening spell in High Eirl.

"Open this box, that I might claim that which is mine by right," she intoned. "By the power of the Fighdrui, I summon the author of this book to hear me and grant me this request."

The material surrounding the book glowed for a moment, then the almonite covering parted into two halves and slid down into the table on which it stood and the Book stood open to the air for the first time in centuries. Gently, Maeve took the book from the stand and carried it over to the table with her things. A few moments after doing so, the almonite once again rose and covered the now empty area.

Checking her timekeeper, Maeve realized she had time to eat and to study the book for a bit before she had to head out and start the journey back. From her tote she brought out some travel rations, and a container of good spring water. Settling back into the chair, Maeve brought the book closer and, carefully, so as not to get anything on the pages, began to read.

Chapter Two

THIS JOURNAL IS THE property of ArdRighian Tara, Ruler of Eirlandia and the Vikes. I wish to write down how I came to this place and time so that future generations may learn from my mistakes as well as my successes. Therefore, I begin at a time when I was only the princess of a minor kingdom in Eirlandia; the daughter of a minor Righ who worried more about his people than was normal for his time.

My father, Righ Eduar, was not a warlike man. Unfortunately, this ultimately meant that his kingdom was often raided by the Vikes, as his army was not as large or strong as the surrounding kingdoms.

We were a fairly poor kingdom, our wealth being in sheep and cattle rather than good land or trade goods. Therefore, we traded peacefully with the other kingdoms and no one thought to invade us.

The Vikes, however, raided us for our animals, which they would use to feed their crews on their raids, then sell the hides to their own people when they returned, for our animals were prized for their fine skins which could be worked and used for many things.

My father and elder brother were away on a diplomatic mission to a neighboring kingdom when Alaric and his men arrived. I learned later that they were attacked and killed while on that mission by renegade Vike raiders. Hence I was the only heir to my father's throne at the time of my capture, but that is getting ahead of my story.

It was, as I recall, a lovely spring day; the kind of soft, gentle day we often got that time of year. It was a good day for doing many things, and a fine day for raiding. And that is exactly what the Vikes did on that day; raid the town of Glin, where I happened to be conducting minor court in my father's absence.

The watchmen, I can only assume, were either not at their posts or had been killed by advance raiders, for we had no warning of the approach of the ship. Our harbor on the Shenon is small, but with enough draft for a warship. I was aware of trouble only when one of my guards came bursting into the courtroom, his face bloodied and his outer tunic torn.

"Raiders!" he shouted. "Raiders in the town! Run, my Lady, hide! They are taking slaves this time!"

"Slaves?" I repeated, feeling confused. "The Vikes never take slaves from here! Are you sure?"

"They have already taken over a dozen!" he answered. "They are only taking women, mostly young ones. My Lady, you are exactly the right age for them to want, judging from the others they have captured. You must go and hide! You are the princess, our ruler in your father and brother's absence. Go! Now! Use the tunnels!"

My heard started pounding. Raiders taking slaves? This was unheard of! A moment later I was out the door, running down the hall and shouting for my maid to gather some clothes and food and meet me at the entrance to the tunnels. I heard no reply but, in my haste, thought nothing of it.

When I reached the door that led to the tunnels, however, I was met, not by my maid, but by a Vike warrior, in full battle dress. He was tall, taller than most Eirlandians and, I suspected even then, most Vikes. His long brown hair was braided and his strong arms and legs visible because of the short tunic he wore. His eyes were also a dark brown, but his face, to my surprise, was mostly clean shaven, except for a long, braided beard.

"So the little eaglet tries to fly away" he growled in Eirl, somewhat to my surprise. "Good thing I was told about this back door; or our main prize would have gotten away!" So saying, he started toward me. I turned to run, but found the way blocked by another Vike. This one was younger than the first, with braided blond hair not quite as long as the first, and he was completely clean shaven. His battle dress seemed made of finer, richer material, and I wondered if he was a superior to the first, despite his younger age. The second warrior's eyes were a blue grey, and seemed to twinkle a bit, almost in glee. 'This is a game to them,' I thought. 'Well they will soon find out how serious this game is.' Seeing no way around them or out of the chamber, I reached down quickly and drew my dagger. I could not let them take me, at least not without a fight.

"Oh, ho!" said the second warrior, "so the little eaglet has talons after all!" He started casually toward me. "Let's see how well you Eirlandian women fight." I made no move, so he taunted me saying, "Come on, eaglet, or are you really only a dove in disguise?"

Although not exactly dressed for fighting, I took a stance and waited. The Vike approached slowly, but did not take out his sword or even a dagger against me. I was relieved he did not bring out the sword, but a little miffed he thought he could take me completely weaponless. "You will find out how well we fight soon enough" I said softly. "You may find me harder to subdue than you think."

So saying, I reached back with my free hand and undid the clasp to my overdress. It fell quickly, and I stepped out of my encumbering skirt. I was dressed now only in my tunic and trews, which I always wore under my skirts. My father, although not warlike, had made sure I knew how to defend myself. There were always brigands about, and as I liked to ride and otherwise have my freedom, he had me taught alongside my older brother. This proved advantageous for me since I knew how to defeat a person larger than I, and as well trained.

The other Vike chuckled. "Looks like your eaglet came prepared, Prince Alaric," he said, again in my language. "You had best watch out, I hear some of these women are decent fighters."

"There hasn't been a woman born who can best me," growled Alaric, this time in Vik. "But I will be careful, Sven, as I don't want to damage the merchandise." Then he suddenly leapt toward me and all became a blur.

I dodged his charge, and hit his back with the hilt of my dagger as he passed. At the time I wished I could have gotten the blade into it, but it had happened too fast. Whirling, I feinted a swipe at his face and got some space between us. The other man, Sven, simply kept out of our way, watching intently.

Alaric recovered from his failed attempt, and turned quickly, grabbing at my wrist, but missed. Growling softly under his breath, he came at me low, then suddenly stood upright and swept his foot under mine. I went down and tried to roll, but the chamber was too small, and I found myself hard against one wall with no room to maneuver.

Alaric simply stood over me, prudently out of reach of my dagger, grinning. "Not bad, little eagle", he said, again using my tongue. "If the room had been bigger, I think you might have gone on for several more minutes before I got you. But caught you I have, and you are mine now by right of conquest. You can come quietly and with dignity or you can try to fight, in which as I shall disarm you, tie you up and haul you out of here over my shoulder. Which shall it be?"

I glared at this arrogant Vike with malice. How dare he speak to me that way! "I am of royal blood," I said quietly. "I will not be manhandled by anyone for any reason. I will come quietly and with dignity. But I give no promise of not trying to escape if the opportunity arises. You are not Eirlandian, you do not deserve my respect."

Alaric looked at me with hard, grey eyes. "So be it, BanRigh. In this land you actually outrank me, not that it matters. You may be ruler here, but you will not be where you are going."

"I am not BanRigh", I protested. "My father is Righ and my brother Tanist before me. I am in line should anything happen to them, but I am not..." I trailed off, for he was looking at me in a strange, almost sorrowful, way. His grey eyes suddenly seemed softer, like the rain clouds on a soft day. His face seemed less harsh also. He stepped a little away from me, so I could sit up.

"Your father and brother are dead, Tanista Tara" he said, gentleness suddenly in his voice. "They were killed yesterday in a raid by other Vikes not allied with me. We are getting out of here, with you, before any of your people find out and raise the army to come to your aide. You are BanRigh, but you will never rule here." So saying he took my arm and pulled me to him, taking the dagger from my nerveless fingers.

I didn't struggle; I think I was in shock. 'Father! Elmond!' I thought. "Dead?" I repeated softly. "Dead?"

"Dead." He agreed. "Their escort, what is left of them, make their way here with the bodies even as we speak. Therefore we are taking ship with the tide and will be well away before they can do anything." He picked up my overdress and handed it to Sven. "Keep this" he said. "I will send men to find other things of this size and type before we leave this land. But right now we need to get the Tanista and ourselves out of here. Go through the back chamber door and make sure it is clear."

Sven nodded and opened the back door that led under the walls of the town and out to the dock. Alaric turned me around suddenly while he gagged me and threw a piece of cloth over my head. "I cannot risk you getting loose," he told me as he bound my wrists behind me. "No one will see you or, if they do, know who you are in those trews and with the hood. The gag will keep you from crying out. I will release you once we are on my ship and away from Glin." So saying, he hustled me down the tunnel and, after seemed like a long time, but probably wasn't, up the walkway to his ship.

Once onboard, Alaric handed me over to someone else who took me to a room and sat me down. He did not speak to me, but I heard his voice softly speaking to others, so I knew he was male. He made me comfortable, but did not remove my hood or bonds. From my seat I heard the sounds of the ship being readied, and felt the movement as they pulled away from the dock. I waited in silence, not sure if my guard was still there or not, as I had not heard the door open and close again. It was some time before I heard the door open, and the cloth was removed, along with my bounds and gag.

Alaric stood there, cleaned up and finally looking like the Prince someone had named him.

"Well, Tanista, I hope your wait wasn't too bad," he said grinning. "We are well away from Glin, and will be stopping along the coast sometime tomorrow for a little while before we head to Vikland."

I said nothing, so he continued, although his smile slipped just a bit. "I assume you wish to freshen up and then take some food and drink?" he asked. I nodded, still not speaking. "There is nowhere you can go to escape here, so you may have the run of the ship, except the cargo holds. You will have a personal guard, as some of my men do not understand that you are not to be touched by anyone. Your guard will also be your guide and will get you things as you might desire them. Do not set foot outside this cabin without Vilk."

He gestured to a small, young-looking man I now saw standing by the door. I assumed he had been the person with me before Alaric arrived. "Vilk may look small and young, but he is a seasoned warrior and my men respect him. He will be your constant companion unless I am with you. Is that clear?"

Although Alaric spoke in a mild voice, his intent was clear. Disobey and there would be harsh consequences. "I understand", I answered. Until we reached a harbor again, there was little I could do. Perhaps I could make Alaric think I had resigned myself to my fate and catch him off guard. I was a good swimmer. Close enough to a shore, I could dive off and reach land before they could recapture me. I was confident I would not stay a prisoner of the Vike for long.

The rest of the day was spent going through the clothes Alaric had brought on board for me. Interestingly, most of them fit, although only a few were actually mine. There were also some clothes of a completely different design than what I was used to, and I could only assume they were Vike clothes. I put those in the bottom of the chest I had been provided, with luck I would never need them. The fancier dresses went on top of the foreign clothes. I kept the workday clothes and night things on top, along with a few pairs of shoes, trews and hose he had also provided.

Once all was arranged to my satisfaction, I asked Vilk if we could go topside for some fresh air. He nodded and gestured me out before him. I knew he could speak, for I had heard his voice, but he spoke not one word to me that whole first day.

Once topside I went immediately to the rail, but saw only sea and a small smear on the horizon that could have been land. Almost immediately, Alaric was beside me. "That's the coast", he said, "but we have a ways to go before we need to land again, so we have put out beyond the range of your people's pursuit boats.

"Come with me, supper is ready; I was just about to come get you." So saying he took my arm, gently, and escorted me inside and down some stairs to the eating area. "I don't usually eat with the crew" he told me on the way down, "but I want to formally introduce you and let everyone know that you are not to be trifled with in any way." At the bottom of the stairs he stepped before me and walked down a short corridor and opened the door.

The smell of unwashed bodies mixed with food almost overpowered me. Alaric was clean, and Vilk and even Sven had no horrible odors attached to them; but the crew smelled of dirt, salt, mead, whiskey and the gods only knew what else.

Mixed with their stench was the smell of onion, fish and other cooking odors. I coughed and my eyes began to water. Alaric looked back at me sharply, and I blinked and swallowed. I would not have his men see me weak in any way. Seeing my reaction to his look, he smiled thinly. He knew, I think, what I was thinking and approved.

The room was crowded and noisy, but Alaric simply stood a moment at the doorway and a Greater calm and silence suddenly descended. Even the noise of the cook stopped for a moment. Then, like a rumbling, there came a sound from the men. "Al-ar-ic, Al-ar-ic!" they chanted. "Alaric, Alaric, Alaric, Vike, Vike, Vike!" They continued growing louder. Alaric just stood there another moment, then put up his hand for silence.

"Good crew! My brave men, my hearty Vikes, I give you greetings and bless you in the name of the All-Father as your prince. We came away today with much loot, several slaves and a very special prize, a Tanista of Eirlandian blood. Our raid was a great success, and my father will be well pleased with all of you. Woodooen has surely blessed us and you will share in the spoils, all the spoils, but one."

As he said this he reached behind him and grabbed my arm, pulling me around and in front of him. "This is the spoil you may not have. This is Tanista Tara, former princess of the Killbrae and destined to be BanRigh of her tribe, but now she is mine and will not be a BanRigh of the Eirlandians, but Truwif to me, Alaric, son of King Leeife of the Vike! Look upon her and remember her. Treat her with respect when you see her and do not assume that, if she is alone, she is helpless, for she is not. And if she is harmed in any way by any one of you, that one shall swiftly meet Woodooen in his moon house and NOT as a warrior. Understood?"

The men's faces were hard and blank. At first I thought they would rebel. Then Sven shouted "Of course, Prince Alaric. To the Leader goes the best of the spoils. We all know that! Tell us something we don't know! Tara is safe with us as if she were our sister. Now quit scowling up there and sit down so we can eat!" The rest of the men started laughing and shouting their agreement with Sven's words.

Alaric smiled and led me to the table. "Sit, then, Tanista Tara of Eirlandia, and have your first Vike meal."

Chapter 3

Later that evening, as I prepared for bed, Alaric knocked on my door. "Tara," he called through the wood, "open the door. We need to talk."

Wrapping a robe around me, I opened the door. "About what?" I asked. I was tired and in no mood to talk. The supper had been tolerable, but I wanted to be away from all the men, the noise and the smell. I wanted to sleep and then to plan a way to escape back home.

Alaric stood in the entryway, looking both regal and frazzled at the same time. "We will be stopping tomorrow at a safe port, where we will stay for some days", he said. "I need to discuss my plans with you and to obtain your word on a few things. I know an Eirlandian's word is as good as a written contract, and I need such an agreement from you. It will save me much worry and your countrymen much grief and bloodshed. May I come in and sit down? The hall is no place to discuss such matters."

Backing away from the door, I gestured him in silently. I knew very well that this was all face-courtesy, and Alaric would do what he wished no matter what I said or did. Best to get this over with so I could sleep. I had no plans to give my Honor Word to anything, but I could pretend to at least listen and say I would think on it.

Alaric closed the door behind him and went to a small cupboard I had noticed but not touched. Opening it, he brought out two glasses and a container of mead. "Discussions are more civilized with drink to accompany them" he quoted from "The Brehonia", a treatise on manners and hospitality all Eirlandians knew from childhood. So saying he poured two measures and gestured for me to sit in the more comfortable of the chairs in the cabin.

"Tara, there is no easy way to say this", he began. "My mission on this raid was to capture you and some other women approximately your age to act as your maids in Vikland. You are coming as a royal captive, a hostage, to ensure your people behave themselves in the coming months."

"Behave themselves!" I repeated. "What are you talking about? I have no say over anyone's behavior! My own kingdom's people know me, but I am hardly a household word in the other realms of Eirlandia, and certainly am not well known in Kilawey. What does my fate matter to the ArdRigh?"

"You are more known than you might think", Alaric answered. "My father has several men at court of the ArdRigh. They have heard your name spoken around Kilawey many times in past few cycles. They have heard talk that your father was going to be asked to bring you to Kilawey to be formally presented to the High Court and to be sworn as Tanista to the ArdRigh if you and the High Council agreed."

"What?" I shook my head in wonderment. "You are insane! Or your father's men are either liars or mistaken. Why would I be chosen as Heir to Kilawey? My lineage is not that illustrious. I am no relative to Brionston. Why me?"

"What do you know of your mother?" he countered. "What know you of the High Consort?"

"My mother? I know nothing of her, really. My father and brother never spoke of her. She was a foreigner of some sort who died in childbed, my birth, in fact. There were rumors she was Sidheran, but my father never acknowledged that, and my brother claimed he was too young when she died to really remember her.

"I have a necklace that was hers, I wear it constantly. My nurse used to tell me to never take it off, no matter what, because it would protect me always. But that is nonsense; a piece of jewelry cannot protect someone. I wear it because it is the only thing of hers I possess. I am not even certain Father knew I had it. My nurse gave it to me when I turned seven cycles. But she made me promise a High Promise that I would tell no one about it, not even my father, unless, when I was older, I had reason to do so. And this is why I am telling you. So you would know and understand. What has my mother to do of this anyway? And what about the ArdRigh's consort? Explain this to me." I folded my arms and glared at him.

Alaric chuckled a little. "Relax and drink the mead, Eaglet. Your questions will be answered; don't ruffle your feathers at me! I had a feeling you did not know your own family history, hence my question. Let me then enlighten you, something your father was remiss in not doing. I guess he didn't want to dwell in the past, and thought nothing would come of it. But something has come of it, and now it is even more important in light of the death of your father and brother."

I relaxed a bit and took a sip of the mead. It was very good, a product of the Hives of Muenstart, I could tell. The warmth of the drink ran through me, and I relaxed. If Alaric actually knew something of my mother, I would be pleased to hear it. But I wondered just what his words about my possibly becoming Brionston's heir were all about. It still made no sense.

"Now then," Alaric continued, "your mother was, indeed, Sidheran. In fact, she was a Principea of the Sidheran. She was also the sister of your current ArdRigh's consort, and niece of your Brionston's father. It all gets a little complicated and I don't know all the ins and outs of the genealogy, but apparently the Clan Boroumma has had connections with the Sidheran for several hundred years. This fact has been kept quiet by the Bards, so few beyond the immediate family know of this relationship. I guess it all happened during the last Great War between the

Sidheran and the Formorrid. Your mother's clan was outnumbered and would have perished if the Clan Boroumma had not come to their rescue. To honor their help, the Sidheran vowed that they would intermarry with the rulers of Eirlandia and that one day a member of a particular family of Sidheran and a member of the Clan Boroumma would be the catalyst for a wonderful occurrence. You, Tara, from all anyone has been able to piece together, are that person."

I just about choked on the mead. "What? What are you saying? I'm no one special, I promise you. If I had been, why wouldn't my father have told me? Why would he have kept this secret?"

"For your protection, Tara," Alaric answered. There are other clan leaders who would have tried to have you killed if they had known the truth of your family history. You are heiress to a royal Sidheran heritage, and the rulers of both Eirlandia and Sidhera wanted you to grow up safely and in ignorance so that your actions wouldn't accidently betray your ancestry. Also, I don't believe even your father really knew the extent of your parentage until recently, when he received the notice from the ArdRigh to bring you to Kilawey by Bellentaine Eve."

Alaric put down his mead and crossed to me. "I have put myself at great risk in telling you all this", he said. "If others learn who and what you are, I am not sure I can protect you. You are a great asset to your people and greater detriment to ours. If you had reached Kilawey and learned what you needed to and became Tanist, then the plans of several generations of Vikes would have come to naught. This is why the raid on Glin; to secure you before your father could bring you to Kilawey and you could come into your rightful inheritance."

He cupped my chin, but gently. "You are part Sidheran, Tara, and your otherworldliness captured my attention since I first saw you. You have no idea of the effect you have on me. But you are about to find out." So saying, he leaned forward and kissed me, gently at first, but then with greater passion.

Gasping, I started to struggle, but he just pinned my arms and continued to kiss me. My body started to betray me, and I felt a heat in my loins. I had had no man as yet, but I wasn't wholly innocent of the ways of man and woman. I had attended the Bellentaine rites for 3 years, but my father had not allowed me a '*nighting*' as yet, saying I was too young. Still, I understood what was going on, and was furious at my body's response. He was Vike! He was responsible for my father's and brother's deaths! I would Not give in to him! I would not!

"No!" I cried out between kisses. "No! You will not do this! I claim Captive Right! I am the same or superior rank than you; you cannot do this without consent!" Writhing furiously, I finally broke his hold and backhanded him as hard as I could. His head snapped to the side and loosened his grip. I brought up my feet and shoved hard against him, sending him backwards and onto his arse. I stood up, trembling with a mixture of rage, fear and sexual desire. "If I am all you say I am, Alaric of Vikland, then you have no right to treat me as a common captive! Leave here, now! We can continue this discussion when you can behave as your rank requires!" I pulled myself as tall as I could, and concentrated on appearing as regal as possible.

Alaric rubbed his cheek and jaw and shook his head. "I was warned about you," he said sheepishly. "I guess I should have listened a little harder. My apologies, Lady, I let the moment get ahead of my manners."

So saying he inched backwards and stood up. "We will reach our harbor by early morning. We will be going ashore for some time while I await instructions from my father. You will be guarded but not molested, and will be free to explore our part of the Dun as long as you do not try to escape or get messages to your people. We are going someplace where my people hold sway, so you will have no allies to help you. The sooner you resign yourself to your fate as an honored captive, the happier you will be." Rubbing his jaw once more, he turned and started to the door.

"Good night, Tara, I hope you sleep well. You will be served breakfast here in the cabin. I will come to get you when we are ready to depart the ship. Have your things packed neatly and dress appropriately to your station. I will have Vilk bring you the dress I wish you to wear tomorrow when he comes with your breakfast." So saying he opened the door and went through. I heard the key in the lock turning. I was truly a captive for the night.

The next morning, just after sunrise, Vilk knocked and opened the door slightly. "Breakfast," he called, he spoke Eirlandian with a strange accent and syntax, but he was understandable. His voice was low for one so small and young, but pleasant on the ear.

"Yes, come in", I answered. "I have cleared space at the table, you may set it down there."

Vilk came in with a tray in his hands and a gown draped over his arms. He put down the tray and held out the gown. "Alaric says you are to wear this, Lady. You are to have breakfast, get dressed, and make sure you are packed. I will help as you need, I have some experience with women's clothing." His cheeks turned a bit red, but he met my eyes easy enough. "I was a merchant before I was captured many years ago. I would help women customers try on clothes sometimes. Then the Vikes took me, found my warrior skills better than they expected, but also found I was a bit different. I became chief guard for female prisoners, as the Vikes came to understand that I had no interest in women in my bed."

"Oh, I see" I said in a neutral tone. "You are *ardinard*, then?"

"Yes, I am from Greecan, where this is commonplace. Not so much amongst the Eirlandian and Vike I know, but not unknown. Eirlandia at least accepts how I am without fuss. I never stay long in Vikland, as they do not accept so easily."

I nodded and sat down at the table, opening the cover to the dish. It smelled very good and looked very tasty. With no more ado, I broke my fast.

Vilk put the gown down on the bed and tidied up the room while I ate. When I had finished, I rose and washed as well as I could. Then took up the gown.

It was a light green, with scalloping that looked like waves on the neckline, sleeves and hem. Of a soft material I could not place, it was laced on the sides so that the patterning on front and back were not interrupted. Undercoats were already attached to the outer dress, so I had only to slip it on and all was done. With Vilk turned away of his own accord, I slipped out of my sleeping dress and put the gown on.

At a small sound, Vilk turned and did up the side lacings, which I could never have managed myself. He also brushed out my hair and pinned it up in a way I had not seen before, and assumed it was a Vike style. It suited me and the gown, however, so I let it be. I had never been one to believe that because someone is an enemy that their culture has nothing good about it.

Lastly he brought forth some slippers that matched the dress, but were sturdy enough for walking or riding. I smiled and put them on, letting him lace them around my ankle, another style I had not seen. But they were comfortable and handsome and hardly even seen under the gown.

We had just finished, when a knock came at the door. "Tara, are you ready?" came Sven's voice. "Alaric needs to know how much longer you need."

"I must finish packing," I said. "I have only just finished breakfast and put on the gown I was given. Tell Alaric he is rushing things a bit and if he had wanted me ready by now, he should have sent breakfast earlier! However, I should be done packing in about two candle marks. If I am done earlier I will send Vilk to let him know."

Sven chuckled. "Very good. You are more organized that even I would have admitted. I will see you topside shortly." I heard him retreat down the corridor and smiled. Despite myself, I was beginning to like Sven, and I had already decided I liked Vilk. I even was beginning to have good thoughts about Alaric.

"Best be to packing, Lady", Vilk said. "Must be ready on time, or Prince Alaric gets upset."

"Posh on Prince Alaric" I retorted. "I will be on time because I said I would be, I am not afraid of Alaric's temper. He has more reason to be afraid of mine." I looked at Vilk and winked. His puzzled expression told me that Alaric had not mentioned his retreat from my chambers the night before to anyone. "Don't worry, it doesn't matter. Let's finish packing, it is all but done anyway. We just need to put in my night things and my kit from this morning into the trunk and close it. I didn't take anything else out and I had already arranged the other clothes yesterday."

In less than a candle mark I was ready, and sent Vilk to let Sven know. As I awaited his return, I took out the necklace of my mother's. In the early morning light it gleamed palely. Its light blue surface seemed to shimmer and I glimpsed, for the first time, a tiny pattern that seemed to emanate from the center of the stone.

'*There, my love*', I remember Nurse saying that day as she placed the stone around my neck, making sure the chain was long enough to not be seen under my clothes. '*There, keep this stone. It was your lady mother's, the only thing of Sidhera she had. 'Tis a shame she wore it not when you were born, or she would still be alive. Lifenstone, they call this gem, bringer of life and light. Wear this always, and show it to no one, including your father. It is given mother to daughter down a line and has always been so since first the Sidheran walked the shores of this land. It comes from a place and time far, far away where, they say, magical things abounded and the Sidheran knew how to command the elements themselves.*'

I heard footsteps in the hall and quickly tucked away the stone. The voices of my past faded into the voices of my present. There was a perfunctory knock, then Alaric entered, carrying a large cloak and hood.

"Put this on" he ordered. "The weather is not at its best, and I don't want the gown wetted and ruined before we come to the Dun. Make sure the hood is completely up, it will cover your face, but just look down, I will guide you to the carriage and out again. It is good you are ready early, as the journey will take a little longer than I hoped." So saying he helped me on with the cloak.

Chapter 4

There is nothing to tell of the ride to the Dun. I could see nothing and Alaric was quite right about the weather. Wherever we were, it seemed that winter still had its grip on this place. The rain was hard and icy cold and the wind kept threatening to lift the heavy cloak hood right off my head. It did not succeed, but each moment was a battle. The carriage had no window coverings, so the weather blew through the carriage. It wasn't until we were within the shelter of the courtyard of the Dun that the wind seemed to lessen. I could almost feel a force beyond that of simple high stone walls keeping the wind at bay. When I got out, I realized there wasn't even any rain in the courtyard. I tried to look up, but Alaric took my arm and led me forward quickly, and I had to look down, watching my stcps so that the great cloak did not trip me.

Once inside, we hurried into a great chamber, or so it seemed from the echo of our footsteps. Alaric at last stopped and took the hood down from the cloak. I looked around and was totally bewildered. The place looked neither Eirlandian nor what I imagined at Vike stronghold to look like. The walls were a uniformly dark color that did not look like stone, but I could not imagine what else it could be.

Globes filled with some sort of light lined the walls and hung from the vaulted ceiling, although I could not see the chains that held them, nor imagine how one lit or extinguished them from that great height. All this took but a few moments, and I turned my gaze to what lie before me, and gasped softly.

Before me, about fifty steps away, stood a dais made of the same black stone-like substance. On the dais was a throne of dark wood with dark red coverings. What sat on that throne was the strangest creature I had ever seen.

The creature was tall, that was obvious even though it was seated. I learned later it was male, but truly could not tell because of the clothing and the fact it had very reptilian features. Its face, neck and hands all looked scaly, almost fish-like. It had a normal looking mouth, and when it spoke, it did so with no real difficulty. Its words were understandable, but with an accent I could not place. Only several days later did I learn that our hosts were Formorrid, the ancestral enemies of my mother's people. Eirlandians were taught the Formorrid no longer lived, but obviously my teachers were either mistaken, or they lied intentionally.

"Prince Alaric of Vike," the Formorrid greeted, "we welcome you and your men. The identity of your guest had not been revealed. I cannot say we are pleased, but we will abide by our arrangement.

See she is guarded at all times, however, by your own men. Should my people learn of her sojourn here, it could become unpleasant for her."

Not knowing at this point who this being was, I was confused by his words, and by his deliberate snub of my presence. I opened my mouth to protest, but Alaric grabbed my arm and shoved me backwards toward Vilk and Sven, who had accompanied us.

"Emissary Borrdin, I assure you it will be as you say. The girl is our political prisoner and is here only because we could not keep her in Eirlandia and did not have the provisions for an uninterrupted voyage to Vikland. We await only word from my father, and the supplies for our ship, then we will be off. The girl will be kept away from you and your people. She is harmless in any case. She has neither training nor even knowledge of her ancestry. She is no threat to you and yours."

"Be it as you say, Prince" the emissary responded. "Take yourselves now to the guest quarters at the far northern end. You know the way from times before. Your men are there and you may have complete use of that section of the Dun. It includes a private entrance and exit, as you know, and even a garden, although it is still too early in the season for much to be growing as yet." So said he stood and made his way down from the dais and through a door set into the wall to our right that I had not even noticed before.

Alaric looked at me warningly, then led the way back as we had come, turning left when we came to the entryway. Turning, he spoke a single word I could not even begin to pronounce, and the great hall went dark behind us. My eyes went wide, I didn't know anyone possessed magical devices. The ability to create such things was thought lost in the many wars between the Formorrid and the Sidheran. Obviously, though, that part of my history lessons was also incorrect.

Alaric said nothing as he led us through the convoluted route to our part of the Dun. The walls were all the same black substance, but I now wondered if it was stone. However, the identity of the material was not my concern. Not knowing who our host was, I was silently speculating on who would have access to magical knowledge, and what sort of tribe the Emissary was from. We reached the Vike part of the Dun within about a candle mark, I judged, and the walls suddenly went from the black material to normal stone and wood. Opening a large door, we stepped inside a central chamber that looked like it could have been anywhere in Eirlandia, except for the Vikland tapestries along the walls.

Still silent, Alaric motioned for us to proceed across the hall to a smaller door just past the main fire pit. This door led down a corridor to several rooms and ended at another door. Opening that, Alaric entered into a smaller version of the chamber we had left and indicated a door flanked by two Vike guards.

"Your suite of rooms" he told me. "Mine are across the way", indicating another door with another guard at its entrance. "The central hall is where meals will be served and meetings held. Your chambers lead out into the garden the Emissary spoke of. Vilk will accompany you and show you around, he has been here before.

"I will let you settle in, then come to get you within a large mark. You need to meet the other members of my staff and entourage. I will also answer your questions about this place at that time. There is drink and some fruit waiting in your suite. Please do not soil the dress." That said, he gestured to Vilk, who offered his arm and escorted me to my suite of rooms, which were actually quite grand and very much 'at home' feeling. I was going to end up missing them when I left them a few months later.

True to his word, Alaric came for me just before the next Major Mark, and led me into the great hall once more. This time there were many people milling about, warriors, courtiers, women of court and many servants. I even spotted a small group of girls who looked Eirlandian, who were grouped together near a corner, with a Vike guard watching over them. I made the assumption these were the other kidnapped girls and smiled encouragingly at them. If they were who I thought, they would be my personal maids soon, and, hopefully, would find the duty enjoyable. A couple of chairs had been placed at one end of the hall, and it was to these Alaric led me, nodding to various people, but keeping silent. Surprisingly, he led me to one of the chairs and gestured me to sit. Vilk stood beside and slightly behind me in an attitude of vigilance while Alaric took the seat to my left, with Sven to the side and behind him just as Vilk was for me.

Once seated, a gong rang out, and a herald announced "Prince Alaric now sits in council. Let all approach to hear and discuss."

The courtiers, both male and female, and the warriors approached the area.

One older gentleman stepped forward, I felt he was perhaps the chamberlain of this place. He had something of the appearance of the Formorrid I had met earlier, but his features were softer, and I wondered if he were a hybrid of Formorrid and Vike.

He inclined his head toward us both, then straightened. "My Lord Alaric, welcome back to DasDunFormorra. We are honored by your presence and assure you that you and your people will all be looked after in the tradition of our people."

He then stepped aside, taking a place next to Alaric, although he still stood. Alaric stood and acknowledged the man. "My thanks and that of my men, Leifson. I have always enjoyed my stays here. This time I bring a special guest."

He gestured toward me, and I stood, feeling it the right thing to do. "May I present BanRigh Tara of Killbrae, unconfirmed Tanista of Eirlandia and last female of her Sidheran mother's line."

A low murmur, dark and somewhat threatening began. Alaric held up his hand, and silence returned. "Tara is my captive, and my father plans for her and I to be hand-fasted before Freyatine. Thus we will have claim on the very throne of Kilawey!"

I stood rooted to the spot in shock. Hand-fasted! Against my will? Claim to Kilawey? The Vikes were mad! No Eirlandian council would confirm me as heir with a Vike mate! What was his father thinking to even propose such a thing? Were they that ignorant of our laws, or just that pigheaded to think we would give in to such a travesty without protest or rebellion? I turned my head to glare at Alaric, but he did not even look at me, just continued his announcement.

He told the people that I was guest-sacred and was allowed the freedom of their part of the Dun, but that I was, under orders of the Emissary of the Formorrid, not to set foot in any other part of the complex. I was not to be harmed, but turned away from any of the exits to the Dun unless he, Vilk or Sven was accompanying me.

He also confirmed that the other girls captured at Glin were my personal body servants and that they were not to be molested or harmed in any way and that the penalties for doing so would be swift and severe. "If we are to convince Kilawey of our honorable intentions, we must treat their people with respect. I will tolerate no disobedience in this matter," he concluded.

Then he turned to the girls and beckoned them forward. "You have come from Glin and, hopefully, know your BanRigh. We tried to pick you so that she would have people who knew how to cook her food, dress and prepare her, make and repair her clothes, and provide companionship. If anyone here tries to harm you or even make a fool of you in any way, you are to tell Sven, my steward, immediately. I assure you that no harm will come to you because of it." He indicated Sven, who bowed to the assembled women. "And now, Ladies, please bring your mistress to her suites. Vilk, her steward, will show you your quarters. Have her prepared for formal supper one candle mark after sundown."

He turned to me and bowed, smiling sardonically. "My Lady, I leave you to your women to rest and enjoy the rest of your day. I look forward to your company at supper."

Oh, I knew how this courtly game was played. I could say nothing in this place and at this time, but he would hear from me my thoughts on this little game. "As you wish, my Lord Alaric. I look forward to our future discussions regarding all this. Mind you these words as I leave, 'Beware setting a trap for the unknown prey, for they may end up being more than you bargained for'."

So saying, I swept regally, I hoped, from the hall with Vilk before me and my ladies behind me. At the door I glanced back and was rewarded by the sight of an obviously confused Alaric watching me. I followed Vilk and heard the doors to my suite close behind me. At last, and for a little while, I could at least pretend I was home.

Supper that night was interminable. Oh, the food was good, a mixture of both Vike and Eirlandian dishes, and the mead was excellent. But I felt as if I were wearing a mask or a costume. The dress I wore was even fancier than the one I had on earlier, and was very heavy. I longed for the freedom of my trews and over skirt, which was about all I wore at home, except for state dinners.

Then again, this was pretty much what this was, a state dinner. Everyone came to gawk at the Eirlandian BanRigh. Even though I had not been confirmed in that title, and probably never would be, these people seemed to think the title was mine. Both male and female courtiers attempted to draw me into conversation, but I simply nodded and kept pretty much silent the whole time, listening to Alaric as he spoke of military matters with, I assumed, a commander of a Vike fleet.

He spoke in Vike, and I am sure he did not know I was actually reasonably fluent in the language. I doubt his spies had reason to know, since I took pains to never betray my knowledge of it to anyone but my tutor, whom I had begged to teach me, saying that it was best to learn the language of the raiders so that we could better bargain with them when the time came to sign the peace treaty I hoped would some day occur. I also had good knowledge of High Eirl, the first language of our people now only in use by scholars who labored to translate the old writings of our ancestors, and those of the Drui who, it was rumored, practiced the arts of the Sidheran in their secret caves and towers, far from others. Still, I had always been fascinated with the language, and figured it might come in handy one day. Just how handy I had yet to learn.

At last the dinner was over, and Alaric rose taking my hand and lifting me also as he did so. "Good people, we bid you good night. The hosagge (a word I knew meant hostage) is no doubt tired. I will accompany her to her quarters and stay awhile. Please, continue your refreshment and entertainment. I will see you for council tomorrow one mark after first meal." Then he escorted me to the suites and dismissed my women.

Motioning me to a chair, he poured himself some more mead that had been left out and settled himself on a stool. "I am sure you have many questions, Little Eagle," he said. "Ask away. I wish you to fully understand what is happening before we leave for Vikland some weeks hence."

I had remained standing, almost trembling with suppressed rage. "How dare you!" I almost shouted. "How dare you show me off like some prize antlerres and have the audacity to proclaim we will hand-fast before Freyatine, whenever that might be. Do you think I am going to agree to this travesty? And do you really think Kilawey would ever confirm me as Tanist after they find out I contracted with a Vike? Are you and your father delusional? Insane? Or just completely prideful to the point of not being in touch with reality?"

Alaric looked nonplused, as if this reaction was completely outside of his expectation. "I am my own person," I continued. "I decide who has thigh-right, no one else. Not you, not your father, not even my ArdRigh. I will Not marry you! I will marry for love, and for no other reason. My father knew this and respected it. If I am to be the ArdRigh's Tanista, I will find someone to be my consort whom I respect and love and who will understand the privileges and duties of a consort, which you, as a Vike, could never understand!" I was in a high rage now, and did not see Alaric's eyes begin to harden, nor his bemusement turn to anger of his own. "I may be your pampered prisoner, Prince Alaric, but I will never, ever be your partner. I owe that much to my people. I will not betray them and grant you a foothold Eirlandia, no matter how precarious!"

"Enough!" Alaric suddenly roared. "I have had enough of your temper, woman. You are my prisoner, as you so admit. As such you are under MY laws. I do not need your consent to hand-fast with you. You are actually already mine under Vike law. You are *breewif,* a wife by conquest. I make you my *Truwif,* my true wife, by the hand-fast ceremony. If you do not wish that, so be it. But your rights as an Eirlandian are no more while you are here or when you go to Vikland.

"Our women do not have 'thigh-right' as you call it. They do as their husband commands, and give their favors to none but him. If we hand-fast, then when we go to your ArdRigh with terms, your status will be greater and you would be in a position to help your people."

Alaric, drew his hand across his forehead, sweeping his blond hair from his eyes. He continued, "We would contract, at least at first, for only the Anu, the one year. That will be enough time for my father's plan to come to fruition anyway. Once our plans are done, whether or not you are my Truwif will make no difference."

He stood up and crossed over to me, grabbing me to him, holding my hands tightly so I couldn't get away. "But know this, Tara, I intend to have my rights of you within a moon cycle, when Bellantine occurs. We will not hand-fast until Freyatine, which occurs after the Eirlandian celebration, as our time of planting occurs later than yours due to our more Northern location." He let me go, and I almost fell. "I wish peace between us, Tara, peace between us and our peoples. This is what this is all about. You can either be part of the process or not, it is your choice. I suggest you sleep on it."

Then he turned and walked out before I could gather my wits enough to say anything else. I stood in that room and cried silently. I cried for my father and brother, for my land, and for me.

Taking out my mother's pendant, I whispered to it softly, in High Eirl. "Oh, mother, I wish I had the legendary power of your people. I wish I could know what is best for all right now, instead of figuring it out as it happens and making, perhaps, the wrong choice."

The stone seemed to glow for a moment, becoming a little bit brighter, then it dulled again. But, somehow, I felt more calm and at peace. "Mother?" I whispered again in old tongue. "Are you somehow here?"

The glow of the stone reappeared, even brighter, and suddenly a beam of light shot from the stone and coalesced into a vague shape about 2 feet from me. "Daughter", I heard a female voice say from the shape, "at last you have learned how to call forth the wisdom of the Lifestone. Hear me now well and remember. You have much to learn and scant time to learn it."

I sank to my knees and then sat on the floor, cross legged. My sight of the present dimmed, and I suddenly found myself walking paths I had never seen, but that looked familiar. My mother was there, I knew it was she even without being told. She taught me about my Sidheran heritage and abilities. I will not go into details in this journal as the secrets are not for outsiders to know. Suffice to say I learned several lifetimes' worth of wisdom, knowledge and magical power in the space of a few hours. This knowledge helped me to change history and create the twin Ruling Crowns later on, along with the other tools that were used in the course of my reign.

I awoke from this strange state around four large candle marks later feeling strangely refreshed and calm. Still, I couldn't stay in this dress forever. I went to the inner door of the suite, and opened it. Spying Vilk on duty, I gestured to him to come in. "I was deep in thought and lost track of time" I told him, somewhat truthfully. "Please help me off with this dress. I wish to sleep." Vilk nodded and quickly had me out of the cumbersome gown.

He turned down the bed and indicated the dressing gown and robe. "May your dreams bring you peace", he said softly. He looked at me in a strange way, then went back out the door.

I slipped into the dressing gown and climbed into bed. The feel was strange but comfortable, and I was soon fast asleep. I know I dreamed, but have never been able to recall exactly what I dreamed. I awoke feeling very refreshed and full of knowledge and confidence I did not have the previous night.

I suddenly knew that I was fated to be Alaric's mate, and that this fate was not so harsh as I had believed. I had a duty to my mother's people, and to my father's people also, and even to the Vikes. Only through a mating between myself and Alaric could the destiny of my people and his be accomplished.

Chapter 5

I AM SURE ALARIC WAS very confused by my behavior the next several days. I was unfailingly kind and courteous. We had conversations that did not end in arguments or even disagreements.

Alaric told me much of life among the Vikes, their laws, their religious beliefs, and their attitudes toward women. It was only the last that I had a problem understanding. Women among the Vikes were not treated equally, and did not have the same rights under law unless they happened to be a widow with no sons. Women could be warriors only if they stood beside their husbands to defend their land, or opted to go raiding, but since women were usually not wanted on board Vike ships, that usually only happened if either the commander had a wif who wished to go raiding, or he managed to find a crew that had several wifs who wished to participate. Not a frequent occurrence.

In response, I told him about my childhood, and about the life and laws of the Eirlandia that he did not know. After all, although he had heard reports from this father's spies, they were not likely to go into everyday life, nor would they know all that much about the law and women's rights. We spent much time in lively but respectful debate about the Eirlandian laws regarding the rights of females. Alaric actually came to admit that our laws made better sense in many ways.

During this time he was also gentle with me, and even seemed to care a bit for me. For my part, I did what I could to let him know I was not opposed to some intimate contact, although I was not yet ready to be *nighted*.

One day, while sitting together in the garden looking at the first budding of the trees and the first shafts of flowers, Alaric suddenly turned to me and took my face gently in his hands. "Tara, I know not what has changed you, but I love the change." He bent forward and kissed me gently on the lips.

That contact caused the strangest reaction. I felt my Lifenstone warm suddenly against my chest, and I felt light headed and almost dizzy. A warmth kindled in my loins and I gasped softly. I put my arms around him and kissed him back, with much more voice and passion than his kiss had been. I felt him stiffen a moment in surprise, but then his arms went around me, and we both lost ourselves in a frenzy of kisses and caresses.

It was only when he undid the stays of my overdress and began to kiss my nipples, that I suddenly put my hands out. "No, Alaric, not here. At least let us have a bit of privacy. The weather is still a bit cold for a romp in the outdoors. And, besides, this place is often frequented by my ladies and your men. I have no wish to be found in a compromising situation." I smiled to take the sting from my words, and gently rearranged my overdress. I stood, and took his hand. "Come", I said, "I know there is at least one room in my suite that no one has spoken for, and I have the only key."

As if under a spell, and perhaps he was, I will never know; Alaric nodded obligingly and followed me to the room. Taking the key from the ring I kept always with me, I opened the chamber door and let him inside, closing the locking the door again. The room was slightly chill, for the fire had never been set, but it was better than outdoors, and the bed was made. Alaric took an extra few covers from the chest at the foot of the bed and placed one on top. "One cover is easier to wash in secret than a whole bed," he said softly.

I stood at the side of the bed, unsure what to do. Part of my mind was screaming that this was wrong, but another part, even louder, said that this was completely right and what had to be done. For the first time in a long time, I took a moment to slip the Lifestone off from around my neck. At Alaric's quizzical look I said, "This is an heirloom from my mother, I do not want the chain broken." He simply nodded, it was obvious jewelry was not something he was thinking of at this moment.

I took the lead and removed Alaric's outer tunic, he followed by divesting me of my overdress. Next came his under chamois, and my inner shift. That left me dressed in trews and my everyday corset. He was in trews only, and his boots. I pushed him playfully down onto the bed and tugged off his boots. Slipping out of my foot coverings, I jumped up and bestrode him, as one might an antlerres.

I played with his chest hair as he undid my corset, freeing my breasts and caressed them gently, teasing the nipples until they stood out plump and pink. I tried to pin his arms above his head so I could have some respite from his teasing, but he was too strong and pushed me backwards instead, swiftly reversing our positions. Holding my hands above my head with one hand, he continued to tease me with other, now taking the nipples in his mouth and tonguing them relentlessly. The heat in my loins increased, and I felt a strange moisture down there. I moaned and tried to turn away to stop this almost frightening feeling.

"Oh, ho, so that is how it is," Alaric whispered. He released me suddenly, and stripped off my corset and trews so swiftly I could not even protest. Then he reached down and took down his trews also.

My eyes grew wide, I had not planned on this!

"Alaric, I don't think…" he stopped my words with kisses.

"Hush, little eaglet, I will not hurt you. This is what your body wants and needs right now. Let me show you the way Vikes perform a *nighting*. I will not go all the way unless you tell me to."

Then he proceeded to start kissing again, starting at my eyes and working his way to my lips, down my neck to my breasts, then down even further to my belly and my loins. My legs drew up of their own accord, and he proceeded to tease with lips and tongue my woman's place until I started to moan and toss. The feeling was both agony and ecstasy, and I was not sure I could take anymore. Then, suddenly, my inner place exploded and I felt myself transported for an instant to the Summerlands.

Just as suddenly, I was back in myself, and I felt a strange languor come over me. Alaric was lying down at my thighs, resting his head on one of them, looking at me with a mixture of awe and gratitude. "My word, I have never seen a First Time, quite like that. Are you all right?"

"Never better," I assured him. "But I do not think we are done. I may have had First Time, but I have not yet had my first *nighting*. I think we need to finish what has been started. Did you not say, yourself, that you would have thigh-right of me before Bellentaine? By my calculations, Bellentaine is tomorrow, which makes this Bellentaine Eve, the night of trysting and of *nightings*. I give you thigh-right, Alaric. I wish to have my *nighting* by you here and now. Come to me, then, know this gift is given in freedom and with love, not by captive-right only."

Alaric shifted position until he was laying beside me. "Given in freedom and love?" he repeated, making it a question.

"Aye, in freedom and love" I replied. "I love you, Alaric of Vikland. I consent to be hand-fasted, and together we will make such a pair as neither of our lands have known". I spoke with conviction, as I was certain I was but repeating the destiny my mother had revealed to me that night. "Do you also give yourself to me in freedom and love?" I asked the question with both hope and despair in my heart. Whatever his answer, I would partner with him, for I had sworn it just then. But I hoped he would answer affirmatively, as then our bond would be stronger and what I was destined to do would be easier.

"Yes, Tara, I to give you myself in freedom and in love. Let it be so before the gods."

And with those words, although he did not know it, Alaric and I were hand-fasted under Eirlandian law. No other words spoken by a Vike Skaald or even an Eirlandian Bard would do anything more than make public this private bonding between us. We were mated, and now we set about consummating that mating. I will say no more on this, for some things are too private for eyes other than the gods.

Chapter 6

A FEW DAYS LATER ALARIC told me that we would be leaving for Vikland at the new moon, which was only two days away. "This is the month of the Mead Moon" he told me. "The moon of marriage. We will get to my father's palace in time for arrangements to be made regarding the hand-fasting. News will be sent to Kilawey, and emissaries from many kingdoms will be invited to the ceremony.

"Frankly, I am not sure we can expect anyone from Eirlandia, but at least we can be on record to say we tried. Please set your women to packing and preparing for the voyage. My father is sending another ship, it should arrive tomorrow. Others of our men who are in line to go home will be on the second ship, which is bringing the replacements. The ship will also carry the extra baggage and larger pieces of cargo that we will not have room for on our ship, since your ladies will not be imprisoned in the hold this time."

I frowned at his jesting tone, and he wiped the smile off his face. "Ahem, yes, well, anyway…" he seemed to lose his train of thought for a moment. "Anyway, I felt you needed to know as soon as possible. I will see you at Day meal?" that the last was a question not a statement made me realize he knew I was upset.

"Of course, Alaric. I will be there. Please send Briggiana in and I will give her the orders for others. We will be ready to leave when you give the word. I will be glad to continue our voyage. I have felt a strange malignancy in the air of this place and will be glad to feel the wind of the open sea once again."

Alaric nodded and left. A few moments later Briggiana, whom I had made by personal valet, entered.

"Lord Alaric said you wished to see me?" I nodded, and told her she needed to start having the ladies prepare for leaving within the next couple of days. I told her what of my things I wanted in my cabin and what others could be sent on the second ship or in the hold as was needed.

When she left to begin the task, I walked to the window and opened the shutters. Looking up, I saw the day appeared cloudless, but there was a strange haze about, and nothing seemed clear. It was almost as if there was a slight fog on everything. My necklace almost seemed heavier than usual. Sitting down on the window seat, I took out the stone. "What is going on?" I whispered in Eirl. I had found out that first night that the Lifenstone only responded to questions in that language.

No vision appeared this time to my question, but a small voice, I believe that of my mother's, answered inside my head. *"The Formorrid are moving,"* I heard her say. *"Borrmid is a Great Worker, and he senses the Lifestone, although he does not recognize it for what it is. Still, he knows that Sidheran mage-power is at work in this part of the Dun, so he is trying to find it. Do not use this stone again until you are out at sea at least one full suntime, so that you are beyond his range of knowing. The Formorrid are formidable, and he could cause you and yours much harm if he decided you were a threat. You must reach Vikland safely and be hand-fasted according to the rites of Alaric's people. Then you must find a way to return to Eirlandia and take up your rightful role as BanRigh of Killbrae. In time, you will have an even greater destiny to fulfill, but you cannot do that until you have much more training; training which can only be completed in Killbrae."*

I nodded to myself and put the necklace away out of sight once more. Alaric had never asked me about the stone. I am pretty sure he did not know what it was or its powers. Indeed, even I did not know the extent of its powers at this point. I mentally imagined pulling a curtain between my thoughts and that of Borrmid.

"You shall not pass this boundary", I whispered to myself in Eirl. I suddenly felt the heavy feeling lift from me and knew that, somehow, my words had become reality, and Borrmid would not be able to track my thoughts and weigh me down any more.

Looking at the candle I realized I had only a few moments before the day meal was set to begin. I did not want to arouse any suspicion or concern with Alaric, so I hurried out the door and down the corridor to the main hall.

The next day proved to be a busy one. I rose early, before sunrise, and got into my traveling attire. Vilk brought in my breakfast, explaining that the captains of the ships from Vikland were meeting with Alaric, and that I was asked to stay out of the main hall until sent for. It seemed that Borrmid was in attendance at this meeting, and Alaric did not want to cause problems in any way, since the Emissary seemed in a bit of a bad mood as it was. It was obvious he was trying to find out something about me, but his veiled questions were all brushed aside by Alaric, who could not understand his concern with me. Alaric had already told Borrmid that he had never seen me do anything strange or out of the ordinary.

"The Emissary was always asking about a necklace," Vik told me, "but Alaric never professed to know anything about a 'strange, glowing stone' as he put it. Honestly, I don't know what Borrmid is going on about either."

I thought about my necklace, hidden away beneath my clothing, with not even the chain visible, and silently thanked my mother for her warning. It was obvious that Borrmid had, indeed, felt the power of the Lifenstone, and was trying to find a way to see it and perhaps even destroy it. I knew that that was one scenario that must never happen.

After breakfast, my women came in and we went through all the trunks, deciding what would come with me in my cabin and what could be safely put in the hold. Then I went for a walk in the garden, knowing I would not be smelling these flowers for many a moon time. The land of the Vikes was much colder than here, I knew, and their flowers and plants much different. I took a few flowers and brought them back into my room, placing the petals in my trunk of under things, hoping their fragrance would linger for awhile.

Just before the day meal, Vilk knocked and asked for my presence in the hall. Borrmid had gone, it seemed, and Alaric wished to present me to his captains.

"I am only dressed for traveling", I told Vilk. "I hope Alaric understands that." Vilk assured me he did, and escorted me into the hall.

Upon seeing me, Alaric stopped his conversation with a tall, bear-like man and made his way to me, a great smile on his face. It seemed my attire was perfect. "Ah, my Lady Tara", he greeted, loudly, causing all conversation to stop abruptly. "All ready for the voyage I see. Good, we leave on the evening tide, but first we will dine with my captains and those men who will stay here to replace those going back home."

He led me to the already food-laden table and sat me on his right. Then he motioned for the other men to join him. As usual, Vilk stood behind me, but

Sven sat today on Alaric's left, in more courtly attire than I had ever seen him wear before.

After the servants had poured each of us some mead, Alaric stood and raised his goblet. "My dear comrades, and Lady Tara, I toast the success of our mission; may it continue to thrive. I give thanks to the Great Ones for their obvious approval and ask for their continued benevolence. Skoolendak!" He raised his goblet to his mouth and drank heartily.

"Skoolendak!" the others shouted back, drinking deeply also. I did not raise my voice, but also sipped my mead, knowing how full and heady it was.

After the toast, Alaric remained standing. "My captains, counselors, friends, I wish to present my soon-to-be Truwif, Tara of Killbrae, BanRigh by blood of that kingdom and unconfirmed, as yet, Tanista of Eirlandia. As no doubt you were informed before you came, we will be hand-fasted come this Freyatine. She is of twice noble blood, being High Sidheran on her mother's side as well as of the bloodline of Ammerigan of the Eirl on her father's.

"Someday, may it not be soon, she may even be Consort to your King!"

"All hail Prince Alaric and King Leeife!" came the cry from Sven. "All greetings to Truwif Tara of Killbrae! May the Powers grant you prosperity and success!" Goblets were raised, and again we drank. I longed for food, as even the little mead I had taken was rushing to my head.

As if hearing my thoughts, Alaric smiled and gestured to the waiting dishes. "Eat now, my friends.

Eat before this mead does its work too well and we cannot enjoy the food. Those who sail with me know their duties after this, as do those whose places will be here. I say only to look to my good counselor, Sheifdar Sven for any advice and last-minute instructions. He sails but a day behind us, but his wisdom is yours for that one day, use him well!" Then he set about eating with eagerness and obvious hunger.

"Ah, Tara, how good it is to finally break fast," he whispered. "That idiot Emissary Borrmid showed up before I could even eat this morning. Since he refuses to eat Vike food, I could only suffer in silence. I thought he would never go away. The questions he asked about you! Insufferable! Why he seems to think you are a threat, I do not begin to understand."

But I knew why the Formorrid was nervous. He sensed my growing understanding of the Lifenstone and was concerned what it might teach me. Little did I realize at the time just how right Borrmid was to be nervous. The power of the Lifenstone was more than I could begin to imagine at that point. In the times to come, I would learn the stone's power, and my own.

Right then, however, I was more interested in the voyage I was about to take than the Formorrid's strange behavior or even the secrets I would someday learn about my past and my power.

"How long to Vikland?" I asked, as I ate some scones and whitefish. "Will there be storms?"

"No storms anymore" Alaric answered, "too late in the season. It should only take about four suns to get to the coast of Vikland. Then we will take another day to travel up the great fjord to my father's stronghold.

Once there we will be parted until the Eve of Freyatine when we will be hand fasted by the Arch Skaald of our land in the presence of all the nobles of Vikland and other friendly countries. Your people will also be invited, as I mentioned, but I don't know if they will send anyone. The Eirlandians do not currently have an ambassador to Vikland, and have refused to have one of our people act as one to Eirlandia. Perhaps this hand fasting will change all that."

I nodded. "Do you think your people will accept me?" I asked softly, not wanting my neighbors to hear. "I don't want to spend my time watching my back for knives or other unpleasant things."

Alaric's eyes grew dark, and his voice was cold, though soft. "We do not harm captives, and you will be special, since you will be a part of the royal family. No one would dare hurt you, and, really, they have no reason to. The Eirlandians are not our enemies, your people simply have things we want and need and it is a tradition in our land to take, not trade, unless taking is impossible.

"You are a high-ranking captive, you will be treated with the deference you deserve and are accustomed to, do not be concerned. Vilk comes with us and has asked to be your personal body guard. If that suites you, I will let him know before we land. It means a promotion for him, so he will serve you loyally.

"Vilk was also a captive, once, but has embraced our way and is, mostly, accepted by all."

He smiled, and I realized he was not angry at me for my question. I had a feeling that he wasn't telling me everything, that the coldness in his eyes and tone was because he knew of someone, or more than one, who would not be happy to see me. But I also trusted Alaric, and Vilk for that matter, to make sure I was not treated poorly.

"What is it like in Vikland?" I asked. "Are there law books or other things I could read before we land so I know how to behave?"

Alaric laughed softly at that, and his eyes grew light and sparkled with humor. "My dear Tara, I want you to behave exactly as you would at home! I want my people to see how the Eirlandians think regarding females. I don't think our laws are just in many cases, though please don't mention that to my father. Your people are right in giving women the same status in all things as men. I have seen your women fight, when they have to, just as well, or better, than their men. I know how shrewd they can be in bargaining, and how organized they need to be in running a household. I think some women would be better campaigners than men! Quartermaster would be a fine job for them! Even heading up a troop, if we could ever get the men to obey a woman's orders."

He smiled sheepishly. "We men will take some training and convincing. But I think seeing you, seeing how you act and how decisive and bold and brave you are will do a lot toward convincing the

Aalders that women have more talent, courage and ability than we give them credit for, much of the time."

I smiled at his enthusiasm. I wished him well on his quest to bring the women of Vikland into equal status with their men. I knew it would be no easy job, and probably would not happen until, and unless, he became King. He might, as Prince-Heir, get some beginning laws passed, but true equality would not happen overnight, nor easily.

Even with laws on the books, the outer settlements would take time to really adhere to the law. It was the same in Eirlandia, how could I expect different in Vikland?

At least in Eirlandia, we had a belief in deities where both the male and female were completely equal. In fact, if anything, the female was considered of slightly more importance, since it was she who had created and nurtured the world at the beginning, and it was through her sufferance that any man partook of her bounty.

Thus it was that the wife had say over when crops would be planted, when animals would be sheared or slaughtered or even hunted. It was women who had some of the highest places in the judging and making of our laws, for they were less prone to bribes and had more of a feel for who was truthful and who was not when telling their side of a story in a court of law.

Ah, well, all things such as this take time, I knew. I could only be supportive and do what I could to help speed the day. Little did I know then that I would be a great asset in helping Alaric achieve his dream; more so than I had reason to even imagine at that point.

Alaric finished his mead and stood. "My captains! Lady Tara! We have much to do and little time to do it. Please, finish your meal, then I would ask you to prepare for the sailing.

"Lady Tara, Vilk will accompany you to the ship when it is ready. I ask that you go now and make sure all is in order. We depart on the evening tide."

Then he abruptly turned and strode out of the room. The others did not seem confused or upset by his behavior, but I was stunned.

'Why are we leaving a day early?' I wondered to myself. 'I truly thought we were going tomorrow'.

Vilk appeared at my side and silently pulled back my chair. I rose and, to my astonishment, so did the men. Nonplussed, I smiled and nodded.

"Gentlemen, thank you for your company. I go now to prepare as my Lord Alaric requested. I was unaware of our earlier departure date and have more to finish than I realized." This, actually, wasn't true, but I needed to leave and Alaric had given me a perfect excuse.

"Of course, Lady Tara", said Sven. "Pleasant day. I will see you off this evening."

He winked, and I remembered that Alaric had said he would be staying on here another day. I hoped he would not be long delayed in joining us. I considered him a friend and ally, and felt I would need all of those I could find when first I landed in Vikland.

I smiled warmly at Sven, then went with Vilk to my suite.

I needed time alone, desperately. My necklace seemed heavier, as it did any time it wanted to communicate with me. I needed privacy for that, however, so I asked Vilk to go check on how the packing was doing, and to return in one large candle mark. Vilk raised his eyebrow at the time request, for he knew that I knew he could find out what he needed in much less time.

But Vilk was very astute, and must have seen something in my eyes that let him know my need for being alone, for he only inclined his head in acquiescence and left.

I locked the door behind him, so that none of my women could just come in unannounced, and seated myself at my favorite seat near the window overlooking the garden. I took out the Lifenstone and held it in my hands. It was warm and pulsating, as if with life. I closed my eyes and whispered in Eirl, "Tell me what I need to know". Then all went dark.

The knocking on my door seemed louder than normal, and I realized it had been going on for a time.

"Lady Tara" came Vilk's voice from the other side, "Lady, are you alright? Can you hear me?" I realized my blackout must have lasted longer than it seemed.

"Yes, Vilk, I am fine," I called back as I stood and crossed to the door, unlocking it. "I'm sorry, I must have dozed off", I said as I let him in.

He looked at me sharply and, again, seemed to read something in my eyes. "Well, Lady, I hope you enjoyed your nap." He said quietly. "All is ready and we must meet Alaric in just a short while to board ship. May I suggest you tidy yourself a bit and then meet in the Great Hall in one candle mark. I will finish some last minute things myself and meet you there."

I nodded and turned toward the wash basin. Looking at myself in the mirror, I could see small lines of fatigue and almost sleep. I had not fallen asleep, of course, but the knowledge the Lifenstone had imparted to me was buried deep inside for now. I knew I had more knowledge than before, but I was in danger here if I tried to recall it, so I let it lie; knowing it would come to me when needed.

I washed and put powder on, to lessen the look of fatigue. Then I put my hair up and put on my cloak, the same heavy one I had worn when first I came in. Alaric had told me it was 'special' and was proof against 'many dangers' and would serve me well if weather should become an issue, among other things. I had a feeling there was, perhaps, more than just protection against weather in the cloak, as my necklace tingled slightly when I put it on, as if in recognition of a sister power.

I met Vilk in the Main Chamber as he had requested and he led me to a small antechamber where Alaric and Sven were discussing something with a map between them.

Seeing me, Sven smiled broadly and quickly curled the map up and away. "Ah, Tara, it is good to see you again. I will not see you until after you are established in the palace. I wanted to wish you safe voyage." He stepped around the table and embraced me as an uncle would a young niece. "You will make a wonderful Truwif to Alaric, and a great consort when the time comes someday. I think Vikland will take to you, and you to it, after a little adjustment time on both your parts." He grinned broadly, as if to some private joke, then turned to Alaric.

"I will leave you then, Cousin, to go to your ships. I will finish up here and leave on the morrow's tide. We will meet again in Vikland, in the shadow of the Father's Eye."

Embracing Alaric, he strode quickly from the room, the charts clutched tight in his hand. I never did learn what that conversation had been about, although I often thought about it in the years that followed.

Alaric stared after his cousin for a moment, then seemed to come to himself again. "Well, then, my lady" he addressed me. "It seems you are ready. So am I and the ships. Let us take our leave of this place and head back home."

"Head to your home, Alaric" I corrected him gently. "I have already left mine, and I dare say it will be a while before I return there." But I smiled as

I said the words, so they had no sting. This was my destiny, so my stone said, and I was ready to meet it.

Alaric smiled slightly and held out his arm for me. We traveled through the Dun, leaving a different way so that we were never in the Formorrid section of the fortress. I was glad of that, I wished to quit this place as quickly as possible and certainly didn't want to run into Emissary Borrdin.

Opening a large door, we stepped out almost directly on to the quay. Five large ships bobbed at anchor, and Alaric led me to the largest one, with a carving of a wolf's head at the bow. "This is my personal ship, The Wolfengaard. She has served me well, and I use her to bring home the greatest prize I have ever secured…you." He looked at me with longing in his eyes, and with pride. "I came to capture a princess, but it seems you have captured me instead. Come, I will show you your chambers." And so I followed him up the gangplank and stepped into another part of my life.

Chapter 7

NOTHING OF NOTE HAPPENED on our journey to Vikland. The country was very different from Eirlandia, but beautiful in its own way. The Spirits of this land were different than mine; wilder, more primitive perhaps, but I sensed a welcome from them.

The Lifenstone was quiet, no warnings or feelings. I remember somehow knowing that it would not speak to me in this place, perhaps it could not. Perhaps we were too far away from Eirlandia and its birthplace. Whatever the cause, it meant I was truly alone. Truly an exile from my home and all I knew. Only my servants remained to me.

Upon arrival in Haernstad, the capital city of Vikland, Alaric departed immediately to take council with his father and the Aalders. Vilk helped me disembark and escorted me to my chambers in the Holmstead or Palace.

My suites were beautiful and generously appointed. My ladies had their own chambers, with one just off mine where a personal maid would sleep.

I hadn't had a personal maid before, but Vilk said that one would be waiting for me.

"We have many other Eirlandian captives, from previous raids," he told me. "Normally these are girls who simply captured the eyes of the men on their raids. They are brought back as house slaves, but are treated more like servants. They can earn income and buy their freedom after seven years, but they are never allowed to go back to their own country, as they might be privy to secrets the Vikes don't want bandied about."

I nodded. We did not have slaves, but I had heard of this custom in other lands. "Your maid will also help you learn our language better. I am sure you know some, but most of our people don't speak Eirlandian, unless they are traders or statesmen or raiders. Many of the court speak a little, but the sooner you learn Vike, the quicker you will be accepted."

I smiled and nodded, not about to let him know exactly how much Vike I actually did know. This would be my secret, for now. People tend to talk more freely when they think they can't be understood. This would work to my advantage. I could get to know what people really thought, and not just what they would say in politeness and courtliness. This would only be of help later on, I was sure.

As if on cue, a timid knock came on the main chamber door. Vilk answered it and stepped back to reveal a petite young girl in her late teens. Her red hair and green eyes gave her away as an Eirlandian.

"Sunshine on your head, Mistress Tara," she greeted me in Eirlandian. "I am Briggent, and have been assigned as your personal maid."

"May the wind be soft and the sun warm", I answered in the formal way. "I thank you, Briggent. Come in and start your duties. My trunks are coming from the ship, but I assume there are some things here already? I could use a warm bath, for one thing."

Briggent smiled. "Of course, my Lady, I have one prepared. This way, please." So she led me off, and Vilk waved goodbye and left.

After a very nice bath, better than I had hoped, I dressed in one of the gowns that Briggent picked out for me and sat down to some tea and biscuits. The food was slightly different than what I was used to, but still homey and comforting.

Briggent started my language lessons immediately, giving me the Vike names for things as she served them. Not wanting to start at square one with this, I told her, in Vike, that I had some rudimentary knowledge of the language, enough for small talk as would be needed in a court setting. I would be asking her about things I didn't know, however. I also told her I wished her to swear that she would tell no one of my language prowess unless I gave permission.

"Of course, Mistress," she answered. "I am yours to command. I feel very lucky to have been chosen to serve you, as do all the Eirlandians here. We are not treated badly, but it is not home. You are a piece of home to us, just as we are to you, I suspect. The life of an exile can be hard, and we are all exiles. I doubt you will every see Eirlandia again."

"We shall see", I answered. "I have reason to believe this place will not be my home for very long, in the grand scheme of my life. I have trust in the will of the gods and the weavings of destiny."

I spent the next several hours getting acquainted with my new residence and the people who would serve me. Vilk was the head of my guard and my own personal guard, but there were other maids and menservants, gardeners, washers, even a designated groomsman to personally care for whatever horses I may choose to add to my personal stable. I was, indeed, being treat as a BanRigh and a Vikland Princess. The realization made me feel more like an exile than ever.

About an hour before sunset, Alaric came to see me. He looked around my chambers with a critical eye, but apparently found all to his satisfaction.

"So, my dear Tara, do the chambers agree with you? Have you met your staff? This section of the Holmstead is to be a slice of Eirlandia for you, as much as is in my power to make it so. You are an unofficial envoy of Eirlandia, you know, as you are the first noble to set foot in Vikland. The court is all agog at your arrival.

"Which reminds me", he continued, "we will have dinner with my father and his inner court tonight. There is a reception planned in your honor. You will meet the full court at the festivities after the handfasting." His eyes twinkled a bit in mischief.

"Technically, I am not supposed to see you after tonight until our hand fasting in a week or so. However, as I pointed out to my father and the Aalders, this is not your typical state marriage and you need someone who can speak both Eirlandian and Vike to help you through this time of transition. So, I can see you, accompanied, as often as state business requires until the morning of the hand fasting.

"I will explain more about your part in that ceremony later. Right now I have come to tell you all your belongings are in the palace and are making their way here. I would like you to dress again in the gown I had you wear when we met the Formorrid. It has been set aside and should be in your maid's quarters by now, being properly prepared. No need for the large cloak, but the dress is of great significance, being the dress my mother wore on state occasions such as tonight's presentation. This is a wordless way of saying I consider you the equal of my mother, and that is a compliment indeed."

I opened my mouth to ask more details, but the words wouldn't come out. Somehow I knew that this was not the time or place to ask more.

"I appreciate knowing the history of the gown," I answered instead. "I will wear it proudly. When should I expect you to come to me for the dinner?"

"Will one candlemark be sufficient? I should like to show you around a bit before dinner. That way I can also tell you about the people you will be meeting at the meal and the best way to get on their good side. Not that you have ever had any problem with that, except for the Formorrid, which I still don't understand…"

Alaric trailed off, pausing as if expecting me to say something. I stayed quiet. I knew exactly why the Formorrid hadn't liked me, but I wasn't about to go into it now.

"All right then," he continued after a moment of silence, "I will come for you in one candlemark." A small knock on my door came then. "See, I will bet that is your maid with the dress. Until then, my lady." He bent over my hand but did not kiss it. Straightening, he went to the door and opened it. Indeed, it was Briggent bearing the dress. He gestured her in, then went out swiftly, closing the door behind him.

Briggent stared after him a moment, then shook her head slightly and approached. "This be the gown I was told you were wearing tonight, my lady" she said in a tone of surprise. "It is not Eirlandian, but I was told you have worn it before and no adjustments were needed."

"That's correct, Briggent. I have worn it before. And you are correct, no adjustments are needed, in fact, I don't think adjustments were ever needed. I remember having no one tailor the gown to me when I first received it, but it fits perfectly." A little nagging thought started trying to find its way into my consciousness, but never succeeded. A gown belonging to his mother that didn't have to be altered to fit me? How strange…

"Help me out of this dressing gown and let's get this on. I only have one candlemark to make myself ready to meet the King and his close advisors. I want to look as regal and as Eirlandian as possible, given the gown I must wear."

Without further adieu, Briggent started to unlace the ties and we began my transformation into the Eirlandian BanRigh this court seemed to expect.

Chapter 8

THE GREAT HALL OF the Court of King Leeife of Vikland was a wonder of stone carvings and rich tapestries. The hall had several large fire rings, which gave off enough heat that the cavernous interior actually was comfortable in temperature for me, since I was accustomed to a milder climate.

Alaric had nodded approvingly at my appearance when he had come to escort me to the hall, but had said nothing to prepare me for the upcoming audience. When pressed, he had merely told me to act myself and to behave as I would have in the court of my father. Silently simmering with both anxiety and anticipation, I swore I would show these Vikes what true royalty was.

Stopping near the front of the hall, I saw that a large throne occupied a dais. A smaller throne was set beside it, with two others on the next level down.

A large man sat on the upper throne, obviously King Leeife. He was of large build, and obviously in the prime of his life. Golden hair spilled in braids down his chest, and a large crown, in the shape of a wolf's head, sat atop his head. He wore a robe of white wolf fur, with large gold chains affixing it to his shoulders. An axe made of steel, but edged in silver, and obviously ceremonial, leaned against the right side of his throne. He was magnificent in appearance, every inch a Vike king.

Alaric stepped forward, gesturing me to wait. He saluted the king, proclaiming loudly in Vike, "All hail Mighty King Leeife. See, I bring the Eirlandian BanRigh Tara, as you commanded. She will be my Truwif come the Eve of Freyatine, in accordance with your wish and decree. I bring her before you now so you may know my success." With that, he gestured me forward.

I crossed the hall and came to stand next to Alaric. I curtsied the exactly correct amount one ruler would to another. If Alaric wished to call me BanRigh, I would act as such. A BanRigh hold no one her superior except the ArdRigh or Righian; not even the king of another land.

I looked at Leeife as I completed my bow, and saw he looked both amused and approving. The others I could catch from the corner of my eye did not seem as welcoming. A few dark looks were cast in my direction.

"Prince Alaric", began the King, in a voice loud enough to carry to the end of the room, I was certain, "and BanRigh Tara, I welcome you both to Haernstad Homestead. I hope the voyage was pleasant for you both and that you, Lady Tara, will find your stay with us pleasant and fruitful."

From the soft sounds of muffled laughter, I understood his last words to be of double meaning.

"Only the High Ones know the future, Majesty" I answered. "I will do my best to see that the seeds of this adventure do not fall on barren ground." There, let them know we Eirlandians can use double meanings also.

Alaric almost laughed aloud, but turned it into a soft cough. "My King, may we have leave to sit? I need some good Vikland mead to wash to the taste of my voyage from my mouth."

The king waved his hand in assent, and we went to the seats set just below him. I looked at the empty throne beside the king. Obviously, the Queen was not in attendance tonight. Alaric saw me looking, and said quietly, "There is no Queen in Vikland right now. My mother is dead, and father has not remarried. I doubt he will, as he loved my mother dearly."

"I'm sorry", I whispered back. "I know the pain of having no mother also."

"Vikland needs the wisdom of a Greater Mother right now. I hope you will come to be that voice," Alaric said softly. "Watch and listen. I know you know more of my language than most believe. Let them continue to do so.

You are clever and intelligent. I need you to be my eyes and ears. Father and I have plans, but there are those who oppose us. In time we will take you into our confidence. For now, simply represent your lands and tell me what you hear that you feel will be of interest."

A servant approached with mead at that moment, and we stopped our conversation. The musicians began to play, and, slowly, members of the court came up to us and introduced themselves and made small talk with Alaric.

Most believed I did not know Vike at all, so would only smile and then speak to Alaric, who would go along with the deception and translate what they said into Eirlandian for me. He would also give quick synopsis of the person's court position when it was not obvious.

After what seemed like a very long time, the King arose and stepped down to us. "Prince Alaric, please do me the favor of allowing me the pleasure of taking your intended for a dance," he said formally. Obviously this was unusual, as I heard rustling and some sharp intakes of breath.

"Of course, my King", answered Alaric, "if the Lady Tara is willing. She is her own person, as are all Eirlandians. She speaks a little Vike, ask her yourself."

His answer caused even more of a stir, but the King merely smiled and turned to me, an eyebrow lifted in query.

"The King does me honor", I answered in Vike. "I will gladly dance, though I am not sure I know the measures here."

The King laughed. "They are easy, just follow the others. They are not so different than some of your own dances, I am sure."

In this he proved right, and I was able to follow the measures of several dances with the King before Alaric came to fetch me again. By that time I was breathless, and took the proffered mead and downed it quickly. I followed it with clear water so as not to cloud my senses too quickly.

After the dancing, food was served. A table was brought before our seats, and dishes placed upon it. The King had a large tray by his throne, and the others in the room gathered around smaller tables that seemed to have just suddenly appeared, almost by magic.

Alaric smiled at my confusion. "The tables are always there, just hidden inside the pillars" he explained. "Folding stools are brought out for the guests to sit upon. This was all done while we were dancing. It makes it appear magical to those who do not know the secret, but it is mostly sleight of hand and good planning and execution on the part of the overseer." I nodded and began eating. I was sure I would discover many more secrets before long.

During the meal, the musicians played softly, so people could converse. After most people were done, small groups started to congregate in various areas, sometimes around a table where someone was still eating, but mostly in the spaces between the tables.

Alaric took this time to point out various court members and their names and titles. He said he didn't expect me to remember everyone, but the more often I saw them without them seeing me, the better I would be able to remember them.

A few more individuals approached the king and us, but mostly we were left alone, although I saw many glance our way. I wondered what they were thinking, and how many I could count as friends, enemies or neutrals.

A few smiled at me, but most had a somewhat haughty expression on their faces. A small group, the farthest away, seemed almost hostile, and I wondered why. Perhaps these were the people who did not want Alaric marrying a foreign princess? I know that we had such in Eirlandia, those who thought only pure blood Eirlandians were fit to become part of the ruling class. I thought the idea stupid. We were all closely enough related already. New blood should constantly get introduced so that our children were fit and new ideas were introduced on a regular basis.

After all were done, the King called the attention of the court. In a very short time, the tables were put away, and the court was seated in the chairs that had been left behind, only this time they were in orderly rows before the king and ourselves.

An open space had been left in the front, and I could only assume that we were going to have some entertainment. Indeed, the king announced that no less a personage than the Chief Skaald would perform this night. A murmur of anticipation went through the crowd. I gathered this was a rare occurrence. I murmured the same to Alaric, who nodded his head.

"Skaald Odine rarely performs in public." Alaric told me. "He is usually too busy with his duties. I believe Father asked him to perform tonight as a special honor to you. He is made a study of Eirlandian history and society, and I believe he has composed a lay in your honor."

"Really," I whispered. "I look forward to this."

Just at that moment, all grew quiet. Looking to my left, I saw the Skaald enter from a small doorway set in the shadows. If I had not been looking exactly where he had entered, it would have seemed he had simply appeared, as he stepped from the shadows into the light of the hall.

Gesturing, the lamps toward the back of the hall were suddenly put out, and only the front area, where he and we were, was left in light. In this light, it seemed as if his robe actually twinkled. I realized that his robe must have mica or some other gem or metal somehow woven into it, catching the light. It was spectacular, no matter the method, and the showman side of my Eirlandian nature approved.

Coming to the front, the Skaald bowed to the king and inclined his head to us. Then he turned and faced his audience.

"Good people", he began. His voice was rich and carried even though he spoke not over loudly. "I come tonight at the behest of King Leeife to do honor to our soon-to-be Princess. As you know, she is of Eirlandia, and I have prepared a special lay in her honor. The Eirlandians are not our foes. Though we have raided their coasts and taken slaves and goods from them, they are not weak, nor in any way beneath us.

"As this lay will tell, they are a strong, noble people, who simply have a different way of thinking and living than we do. They walk the path of peace as often as they can, but they know the way of war also. They are not doves, but eagles. Listen, then, and learn of this people." Bowing, he turned and walked up to the same level as the King. From here his song would project to all of us.

Turning slightly in my chair, I saw he had come to stand next to a large harp. I was astonished. I had not realized that the Vikes had harpers among them. Harperbards were rare even among the Eirlandian, and to find a Vike Skaald with the skill…well that was nothing short of amazing. Still, I had yet to hear this man. He might just pluck at the strings once in a while, like any apprentice bard, and tell his tale mostly in words. I was very wrong about the skill of Skaald Odine.

I will not attempt to recite the Lay of Eirlandia here. It was much too long and complicated. I have had the music and words written down in the court documents for any who might wish to read and attempt to perform this work.

For any who do so, I wish you luck and the skill of the Mighty Ones, for that is the only way you will do justice to it.

Skaald Odine's skill was beyond amazing. His voice was able to take on textures and richness I had only heard about, but never had the opportunity before to witness. His skill at the harp had to have been second only to the legendary Amarigin of our country's ancient past.

Truly he placed the history and great deeds of my people before this audience with faultless skill and showmanship. I was speechless and in tears at the end of the piece, which was a very long one indeed. Glancing sideways at Alaric, I saw he had appreciated the lay as much as I, although he was not, of course, as emotionally moved by it.

Prompted by something I could not identify, but that felt like almost a command, I stood, after the applause had ended, and took off a small but very valuable pin I had found amongst my jewelry that very afternoon, deciding at the last moment to put it on.

Turning to look upward and behind me at the master musician, I said, in loud and ringing Vike, "Good Master Skaald, I thank you. I do not have much with which to reward you, but I pray you accept this small gift, that comes from the land you have just now so wonderfully praised in your lay." So saying, I held out my hand for the Skaald to receive the gift.

The man looked momentarily surprised, and I wondered if I had committed a breach of etiquette. But I saw the king smile and nod, as did Alaric. Odine came down the steps and opened his hand. As I placed the pin in his palm, my Lifenstone suddenly grew very warm and reassuring. I knew then that this skaald was going to be very, very important to me here in Vikland. I had an ally, and a powerful one, I somehow knew instinctively

"BanRigh Tara", Odine said, in ringing tones as he slipped my pin on to his cloak, "I accept with gratitude your gift and assure you, in the presence of this company, of my complete and unwavering support and friendship during your stay here with us."

The small, almost unheard, gasp I heard from some in the hall confirmed my thought that here, truly, was a powerful ally and possible friend. That said, the Skaald bowed once more to the king, then to Alaric and myself, and left the hall.

The lights in the lower part of the hall came to life again, and king gestured for more wine to be served. As we drank, a troop of acrobatic dancers came in. The rest of the evening was filled with talk, drink and wonderful, light entertainment.

As it grew later and later, I found myself almost dozing.

Suddenly the king stood, and all went still. "I will retire now," he announced. "So, too, shall my family. If you wish to stay, please do so. Our new family member is tired from her journey and needs to rest."

At this, he came down to Alaric and myself and put out his arm from me to take. Smiling, I took it, and walked with him on my left and Alaric on my right down the hall and out the door, all the while feeling eyes upon us that ranged from thoughtful to angry to hopeful to amazed. My first formal day was done. There would be many, many more to follow.

Chapter 9

I HAD MANY ADVENTURES THE first few days of my sojourn in Vikland, but the next major event was, of course, the handfasting.

I remember clearly that the day dawned bright with no threat of storm. I awoke early, as was my habit anyway, and broke my fast with just a small meal. The ceremony would take place at High Sun with a large and elaborate feast and celebration after. The ceremony would be fairly small, with the Chief Skaald officiating and only select members of the court in attendance. For this I was glad. I knew enough Vike to know that I could understand what would be said, and so was not concerned about that, but I was nervous enough with the thought of marriage and didn't need to worry about a huge crowd perhaps distracting me at a critical moment.

Briggent entered shortly after I had finished my meal, and led me to the awaiting bath. From there, oiled and perfumed, I was dressed in what seemed like layer after layer of clothing, each with, I was told, very specific folk belief attached.

I will not even try to go over it all, there is no need. Suffice to say the bride is surrounded by protective magic on her handfasting day as it was thought the Aellfa, the demon folk of the cold places, watch for an opportunity to put their hands on the new bride and cause her to become cold and barren.

I was given to understand that successful child birth was actually fairly rare, and that infants often did not make it through their first winter due to the bitter cold.

When finally dressed, in an outer gown of white and gold, with my Lifenstone hung out of sight under my many layers and a large diamond necklace around my throat, I put on my slippers and went to the window of my chambers were I offered up a silent plea to my own deities to bless me and to protect and keep me while in this strange land. I sent a plea, also, for my homeland that had been left without a ruler, and hoped it would be safe and its people protected.

There came a knock on the door, and Briggent answered it. It was, to my surprise, not Vilk, whom I had expected, but Sven, looking the most regal I had ever seen.

"Greetings and blessing on this fair day to the fairest of brides" said Sven as he entered, bowing low. "As you have no male relative to escort you, I begged and was granted the honor of being your champion for this time."

I bowed in return. "I am most pleased and grateful, Sven. I look upon you as a dear friend and am happy to see you once again." Indeed, I had not seen him since I had left the Formorrid Dun.

"Are you ready?" he asked. I nodded, and took his arm. He escorted me through a part of the homestead I had not yet seen, then out to an area that took my breath away. It was a large, open courtyard that overlooked a large bay I knew was called a fjord. But rising just to the right was an enormous, snow capped mountain. I had never seen a mountain so large. And right near the top was what appeared to be a large opening drilled into the mountain right through to the other side, where the sun would obviously shine through on certain hours or days. I stopped cold, my Lifenstone blazing, but not in warning, almost more in recognition of this majestic sight.

"Behold the Father's Eye," said Sven softly. "The sun shines through there at the Summer solstice, which is tomorrow."

He smiled gently. "Come, they are waiting. The ceremony is short enough, and soon you will see your Alaric again."

So saying he led me across the courtyard to a small gate I had not noticed. Opening it, we stepped through to a bower, laden with white flowers terminating at a grotto where I spied Skaald Odine. He smiled and beckoned me forward. As I took a step, I heard the piping of musicians hidden somewhere ahead. The music was somehow familiar, although it was not Eirlandian, but it seemed to have elements of my native music woven through it. I passed by a few people I recognized from the first court presentation, then I was standing before the Skaald.

Out of the corner of my eye, I saw Sven step back, and felt the presence of another on my left. I could not seem to shift my eyes from the Skaald, who was standing quietly in front of me gazing deeply into my eyes. Then I was aware the music stopped and the voice of the Skaald rang out.

"Prince Alaric, BanRigh Tara," the Skaald intoned, "you come this day to be joined before this company and in the sight of the gods and in the shadow of the Father's Eye. BanRigh Tara, as a stranger to our land, you may ask any question you desire without it seeming an affront to our gods or our people. Have you a question?"

I shook my head. In the past few days I had been well instructed on what to expect and the history and meaning behind the rite. Although somewhat different from our ways, the Vikland hand fasting was not completely foreign in content and certainly not in intent.

Skaald Odine nodded, then produced a cord and proceeded to bind our arms together with it.

"As this cord binds you now," he said, "remember that you are bound before the people and the gods from this day forward no matter how far you may be separated in body. The words you are about to speak will bind your lives and souls together until the gods decree otherwise. Know and remember this, for the knot tied today can never be truly severed except by the will of the gods.

"Prince Alaric, please declare your intention."

"I, Prince Alaric Leeifeson of Vikland, do come this day to be handfasted with Ban Righ Tara Eduardotterson of Eirlandia." Alaric's voice was strong and proud. "I proclaim her my Truwif with all the rights, protection, privileges and duties of that position. I give to her my strength, my championship, my honor and my love, for as long as the gods decree."

His voice was not loud, but it carried clearly, I am sure, to all present. There had been a small gasp at his declaration of love, and I assumed this was not normally part of the formula, or, at least, one that did not have to be recited. Considering that many times a marriage of state was a loveless one, at least to start, this seemed a logical assumption.

"BanRigh Tara, you have indicated you understand the rite. Therefore I ask you to please state your intention."

There was an almost audible intake of breath from the gathered as I spoke, in perfect Vike, the response.

"I BanRigh Tara Eduardotterson of Eirlandia, do come this day to be hand fasted, by my own will and desire, to Prince Alaric Leeifeson of Vikland. I acknowledge my rank of Truwif along with the rights, protection, privileges and duties of that title. For my part, I give to Alaric my honor, my self and my love, for as long as the gods decree.

"I also state that I will defend Prince Alaric as my consort to the Eirlandians should we ever return to my homeland."

The sharp intake of breath, including from Alaric let me know my proclamation was even more unexpected than his. Only the Skaald did not seem surprised, but merely smiled slightly and inclined his head, as if in agreement or support.

"Alaric and Tara", Odine then announced "you have declared your intent, and you have been bound in the sight of the gods and your people. Pull now the cords and tie the marriage knot for all to witness. May the gods of both Vikland and Eirlandia bless your union."

At that direction, we pulled our arms back to ourselves, creating a knot in the cord by which we had been bound. We turned and held the knotted cord high for all to see. "Welcome then the new couple. Welcome the Prince and Princess of Vikland! Skool!"

"Skool!" shouted the crowd. "Blessings on the couple!" The king came forward then and presented us with matching rings. We slipped them on each other's fingers, then gave the cord to the waiting servant. It would be sealed in a box and put away, hopefully never to be brought out again until our deaths, when the tie would be undone by the surviving partner, if they chose, to signify the bond at an end. Occasionally, the survivor would not untie the knot, signifying they would not remarry.

That last bit of ceremony done, Alaric and I proceeded back down the aisle and entered back into the large area where I had first seen the Father's Eye. This area was now awash with people, tables, chairs, food, mead and music. I confess I had a few unwatered goblets of mead and can honestly not remember much of the festivities which went on until the sun was very low on the horizon and I was very, very tired. At that point, Alaric got up, announced we were retiring, and whisked me away.

We didn't go back to either of our chambers however. He led me to a carriage and helped me in.

"Sleep a little, my dearest" he said. "We journey a bit to the special wedlock house where we will spend the next few weeks." Alaric pulled me close and tilted my head to his shoulder. He continued, "The house is small, and we will have only a cook, maid and one guard on site. But we are still within the royal enclosure, so will be perfectly safe. So sleep now, it is alright. I understand. You are not used to our mead and having such a long day. Indeed, there will be no night, really, for several months, so you might as well get used to it."

I was so weary, I simply nodded and closed my eyes, thinking only to rest and let the mead dissipate. However, I slept the entire journey there, and awoke again only when the carriage stopped and there was a great rustling, as of trunks being lowered from the roof.

Opening my eyes, I realized that Alaric was no longer in the carriage. A moment later the door opened and my husband put his hand in to help me out.

"We have arrived, Beloved. Come, let us go inside. There is drink waiting." Nodding, and realizing that I was, indeed, thirsty, I took his hand and alighted.

It was still dusk, and I remembered that the sun would not truly set for several months. This was the Season of Allday, the Time of Growing, peculiar to these lands. Still, here I was, and I would have to learn to count hours by the candlemark more closely, not just the sun and the light.

Entering the building, I saw the house servants waiting to greet us. They were all strangers. I greeted each in Vike and accepted a clear, cold liquid to drink from the woman servant.

"Clear water from the goddess' well," she told me. "Drink and be sustained by Freyate, she of the waters and the land." Nodding thanks, I drank deeply, glad it was fresh spring water and not more mead.

After quaffing the liquid, and noting that Alaric did the same, I turned to my husband and said, "I have a need and a desire which require privacy. Will you lead me on, my mate?"

A twinkle in his eye, he nodded then took my hand and led me quickly into a hallway that terminated in an ornate door upon which a beautiful bough of flowers was hung.

"Enter now the sacred chambers of the Bonded Suite. This suite of rooms is used only for newly hand fasted couples. We will have no reason to leave this place for the entire time of our wedcation, for it includes a garden and even a section of the forest should we wish to hunt or simply spend time alone in nature."

At that he pulled me forward and ushered me inside, closing the door firmly behind him.

There is no need to write more of this in this journal. My thoughts and activities are recorded elsewhere.

Chapter 10

MAEVE SIGHED AND CLOSED her eyes. She had taken much longer to read than she had anticipated. The story had engaged her thoroughly, pulling her into the adventure until she almost believed herself to be ArdRigian Tara.

But she knew, from the size of the book, that the information she sought was much farther on in the story. She realized that the sooner she returned and handed the book over, the sooner the researchers could find the information they required and, ultimately, the Crowns.

But Maeve couldn't help but wonder whatever happened to the Lifestone which Tara spoke of. It was not, to her knowledge, with the rest of the royal treasure that had been handed down ArdRighian to ArdRighian in the years between then and now.

"Perhaps we need to find that stone first," she murmured to herself. "If it holds as much knowledge and power as I think it does, it might just lead us to the crowns much faster than whatever Tara has to say in this journal. I wonder if the stone is here in the library somewhere…"

So saying to herself, she marked the spot in the journal where she had stopped and closed the book. Wrapping the book carefully, and placing it in her back tote, Maeve hurried back the way she had come.

Coming to the opening, she realized the light was gone. It was night outside, no time to start back. Sighing, she went into the library proper, and cleared a space where she could prepare a meal and sleep. She had lost a day, but she did not really regret it. The glimpse into the past had awakened a deep longing and even need to find the Lifenstone of Tara. Maeve more and more believed that the Lifenstone would possibly be of more help than even the Book.

"Spirit of ArdRighian Tara, hear me," she whispered. "Lead me on the right journey. Your people need the Ruling Crowns and your Lifenstone. Let me be the instrument you use to once again bring peace to this land." So saying, she ate her meal quickly and went to sleep.

The next morning she awoke early, and ate a few more trail rations. She wanted to be on her way, having lost the time yesterday reading. Still, the weight of the book seemed more than just its physical presence, and she felt a profound need to know more of the story of the Great ArdRighian.

"Later", she told herself severely. "I need to make it at least to the way-cabin. I can rest there and skip forward a bit in the journal. News of the crowns will not occur until she has returned to Eirlandia at the earliest."

Having thus convinced herself, Maeve packed up her few belongings and started out.

As she traveled, Maeve thought about all the things she had read in the personal journal of Tara the First. Little was known of the ArdRighian's life, since her story and that of King Alaric had become the stuff of legend in the following centuries. Much had happened to both Eirlandia and Vikeland in the time between. Both had advanced in both magic and science, and while traditions had continued, life had become easier for the majority of the people. Except for some obvious services, such as those having to do with law, medicine and governance, most people did not have to work, although many chose to simply continue the ancient way of life. Therefore, while not needed, farmers and ranchers still existed; and their homegrown goods were in high demand and commanded great respect. No one actually bought or sold things, but trades were made and services rendered as payment for goods received if appropriate.

Eirlandia was a land envied by many other countries, and also respected. But that reputation was at risk now, as the Formorrid were again raising their ugly heads and causing strife between Eirlandia and Vikland. The peace was still holding, and the current Tara and Alaric were doing all they could to keep the peace. They planned to marry as soon as they could, but the unrest in both countries was making planning such a ceremony difficult.

Maeve had been tasked with finding the original journal so that Tara could retrieve the two crowns for the ceremony. Maeve, through her reading, now understood that finding the Lifenstone of Tara was also extremely important to the fate of both nations, as well as to ArdRighian Tara and King Alaric personally.

Because of all this introspection, the journey to the way-cabin seemed less long than she remembered. Still, Maeve was pleased she had made good time. She would rest here the remainder of the day and read more of the Book. She told herself she would skip ahead to a logical place that at least spoke of Tara's return to Eirlandia.

It was still over two days' journey back to Kilawey, and Maeve was certain she would know where to show the scholars to start looking for the Ruling Crowns and maybe, even, the Lifenstone, by the time she returned to the capital.

After stowing her pack and eating some supper, she took the book with her to the small porch, where the light was good. Settling down on the small wooden chair provided there, she thumbed through the book from where she had ended and left her placemark, in search of a sentence or phrase that would direct her to the correct place to begin reading.

In her quick scanning, she read about the ArdRighian's first few months in Vikland and her growing friendship with the Chief Skaald Odine, as well as the intrigues of the Vikland court and the jealousy of some of Alaric's female nobles, who had imagined themselves as his Truwif someday, not some enemy foreigner.

But the story was ordinary and Maeve imagined had been included to provide guidance regarding the Vikes more than anything else. No mention was made of the Lifenstone or Eirlandia until many chapters beyond where she had previously read.

Then, suddenly, she found what she wanted in a few short words. Pausing, she checked the daylight and found she still had plenty of light left to go on for awhile. So she settled deeper in the chair and began again to read.

Chapter 11

One morning as the world was reveling in the Summer of Vikland, word came to the court that a messenger had unexpectedly arrived from Eirlandia and requested an audience with the King, Alaric, and myself.

I was amazed that the Eirlandians would send such a messenger. I was told he had come under a flag of truth, and proclaimed himself a Royal Bard and under the protection of the Ard-Righ of Eirlandia. The messenger had been given refreshment and was now awaiting our decision on whether or not to receive him.

Alaric and I were seated on our thrones, as we had been about to start the day's audiences. King Leeife, of course, was also present, on his throne one step above us. Upon hearing the news, the king dismissed the entire court, saving only the guards around the walls, who were too far away to hear.

"What say you, Tara?" he asked softly. "Could this be real? Or some sort of attempt to spy or even commit violence."

"No Eirlandian would claim the status of Royal Bard without being one," I answered. "The Eirlandians know I would recognize a Bard by their distinctive garb, a multi-colored cloak with a gold trim. I believe this messenger to be genuine since there is no written message. The Bards are specially trained to memorize long and complicated messages so that they can be utilized between parties in times of war or of negotiation, when a written message could be lost or fall into the wrong hands and be altered or destroyed."

"I have heard of this," agreed Alaric. "The Formorrid warned me to be careful of any strangers who had come the last little while from Eirlandia to this court, even as a captive, as they could be a bard spy in disguise.

"Our Formorrid friends are not happy about our little venture here with Tara and, possibly, Eirlandia. They warn of treachery and dire magics whenever I have the unpleasant experience of speaking with the ambassador."

"Yes," the king agreed. "They are afraid we will ally with the Eirlandians against them, and are especially afraid we might find some Eirlandians who are also Sidheran in heritage. Such as you are, my dear," he added, leaning toward me and smiling. "We already know the Formorrid hate the Sidherans for all they are almost extinct."

He looked at us both for a moment in silence. Then he nodded his head in agreement when we both nodded to him.

"Very well, then" said Leeife. "Alaric, go to the door and bid the guard to have the messenger come. We will see what this Bard from Kilawey has to say. We are not at war with Eirlandia, and I see this as a good will gesture on their part to start diplomatic ties with us. I would rather trade than raid, as Alaric knows, much to the disgust of many of my sea captains."

Alaric got up and quickly crossed to the door, which he opened. A few short words, apparently, were enough to send the door guard scurrying away. Alaric opened the door wider and called some members of the court forward.

Among them, I saw, were Skaald Odine and Sven, along with the Chief Scribe, the War Master, the Spy Master and the Master of the Fleet. This small group followed Alaric to the front of the hall, then arrayed themselves on either side of our thrones according to their prescribed places. These men were the cream of the council and advisors to King Leeife. It was their right and privilege to witness this historic meeting.

Only moments after all had taken their places, and a small table with some goblets placed a short ways back from the throne to provide refreshment for those attending, the doors again swung open and the Court Chamberlin entered, bowed, and ushered in the Royal Bard from Kilawey.

One look told me he was genuine. This knowledge this was due to the fact that I knew this man! He had come from Kilawey to Killbrae bringing messages to my father many times.

Daman was one of the chief Bards assigned to the royal court at Kilawey and his presence alone meant that he was delivering very, very grave and important news indeed. This was more than a tentative first approach to a former enemy because of the presence of a minor former Righ's daughter, this was something much weightier. My Lifestone, which had been quiescent these many months, suddenly grew very warm and heavy. This news, whatever it was, was grave indeed.

Sitting straighter in my chair, I schooled my features to impassivity, as I had been taught. A princess never appeared disturbed or anxious; no ruler did. I might not ever have been a BanRigh in truth, but I had much learning in my father's court and had, indeed, had exactly the same training as my brother, for a good Righ knows the value of a well-educated consort by his side.

Daman approached to almost the foot of the steps that lead to the thrones, and bowed. "King Leeife," he began in flawless Vike, "I am Bard Daman of Kilawey. I come before you with a matter of great urgency and sorrow for the people of Vikland and of Eirlandia. Sorrow, too, for the Princess Tara, I am afraid. I beg leave to tell you my message."

King Leeife nodded, but then said to me, "Princess Tara, know you he speaks truly as to his identity?"

"Yes, my lord" I answered. "I know Bard Daman from his visits to my father's court. He is indeed who he says he is. And no Bard ever proclaims anything but truth. I would hear his words and attend them closely."

Daman smiled just a little at me as I answered the king, again in flawless Vike.

"Say on, then, Bard Daman," the king commanded. "Tell us this news of great urgency and sorrow for both our peoples. For I swear I cannot think of anything that my people would think calamitous to them that may be calamitous to you, unless you are to tell me that the ocean gods have risen and swallowed much your land and mine in a great wave. But I doubt you would have survived to tell me such news had it occurred."

Daman smiled somewhat bitterly, but acknowledged the reminder that the Eirlandians and Vikes were hardly allies, and only barely not enemies. "King Leeife, Prince Alaric, Princess Tara, members of this court, I bring the news that the Ard-Righ of Kilawey, Brionston Boroumma, is dead, along with many of the other kings of the land.

"There was, indeed, a great tragedy; not of the sea, but of the land. The kings were making their pilgrimage to Carenow, the holy mountain, when a strong tremor occurred and the land itself opened and swallowed almost all of the High Court and other pilgrims who were undertaking this sacred journey.

"Eirlandia is in turmoil, and the Drui have determined that this event is part of an ancient prophecy given by the Sidheran long ago. The Drui have proclaimed that Princess Tara, once of Killbrae, is destined to be our High Queen and must return to Eirlandia immediately before civil war breaks out.

"This is, of course, devastating news to Princess Tara, who, once she learns the list of people, will realize that many of her kin have died. But it is also of import to you of Vikland; for Tara must come with us to assume her duties, so you will be denied her presence.

"You can consider this a great opportunity, however, since it is obvious the Princess Tara has ties here in Vikland and will fight for better relations between our nations."

Daman then looked at me, solely me, and proclaimed, "BanRigh Tara of Killbrae, daughter of Righ Eduar, daughter of Neeve of the Sidheran, Tanista of Kilawey, will you forsake this land and this court and come to your home of Eirlandia to begin your duties as Ard-BanRigh? Let me assure you that if you refuse, we will not ask again, for we will journey back to a land that will then be torn by bloody civil war for many years, and, indeed, Eirlandia herself may become no more."

My heart was in my throat, a dead weight. I was dazed and confused and very frightened. 'Brionston is no more?' I thought. 'And most of the other regional kings and the high court? Gone? And how do I fit into all this? What prophecy does he speak of? I have never heard this, but Alaric spoke of this before…'

"Tara", Alaric's voice cut across my thoughts. "Tara, you alone must choose. I will not stop you if you must go, but I will come with you, no matter what the Eirlandians may say. You are my Truwif and a Vike Princess also now. Whatever awaits you in Eirlandia, I would not have you face it alone."

"Aye, Tara" seconded the king. "We of Vikland will stand aside for you. And we will be at your back, for you are one of us now. But we will not make you leave. It is your choice."

My Lifenstone blazed, almost seeming to burn. I knew what I must do, no matter how afraid I was.

Standing slowly, I descended the steps until I was on the same level as the Bard. Placing one hand on my heart and one on the crown of my head, I knelt in front of the representative of the Drui and nobles of Eirlandia.

"By my heart and by my head, do I pledge myself to the people and the land of Eirlandia," I intoned in High Eirl, a language used only in the most formal and solemn of moments. The words were those used by the Ard or Ban Righ upon their coronation. It was a solemn promise before the Land and the Spirits that was unbreakable until death or formal abdication of the position at the request of the people.

Standing so close, I heard the bard's sharp intake of breath. But I do not think anyone else did. Only the Bard and I knew what had just happened and what I had just said. My answer had been given. Now I would see what the consequences were to be.

Chapter 12

THE DAYS AND WEEKS following were filled to the brim with all that had to be done in preparation for my return to Eirlandia.

Bard Daman went back home immediately to get things prepared for me there. Unexpectedly, and to the consternation of the court, Chief Skaald Odine unexpectedly announced he would be coming with us, and no one could persuade him otherwise. He had a good replacement, he told King Leeife, and he felt called by the Spirits to accompany me.

"Tara will need all the support she can get", he exclaimed. "I am the equal of the ArdDrui, and he knows it. I can also act as ambassador from this court, at least at first. Once the crisis in Eirlandia is settled, I will let you know, King Leeife, and you can send a formal Ambassador. Who better than a Skaald to explain the ways of our people to the Eirlandians and assure them we are more alike than different?"

At this King Leeife simply nodded in defeat. "Send your replacement to court as soon as possible," he commanded. "And appear with him before Full Court to hand over your tokens of Office. Then there can be no cries of deception or foul play. Also, let it be clear that you will be the one to explain why you are leaving to whole court."

Skaald Odine simply bowed his head and departed.

Several days later, Odine reappeared at court with a younger, though still at least middle-aged, man at his side. The man wore the same type of clothing Odine had worn that night I first met him.

Word had gone out that a new Chief Skaald would be presented, as Skaald Odine was leaving with the prince and the strange Eirlandian princess, so the room was filled to almost overflowing. This would be one of Alaric and mine's last audience day before our final leave-taking. Odine knew this, of course, which is why he had picked this day.

"My king, my prince and princess, captains, councilors, and Viklandians all", began Odine, "I present to you today, as requested by King Leeife, my replacement, Skaald Freedine.

"Freedine," Odine continued, "has hitherto been in charge of the Skaaldara, our school for aspiring skaalds, but has agreed to take on this position. He has been my trusted assistant and advisor for many years.

"Do not let his appearance fool you, he is older and wiser than his looks indicate." At this statement, a small twitter ran through the court. It seems Odine's age had been the subject of many discussions over the years.

"He will serve this kingdom well in the coming years," Odine continued as if the sound had not happened. "He has my full authority and power as of this moment. Even if I return, at some point, to this land, Skaald Freedine will still be Chief Skaald.

Odine then lifted his head and hands to the sky in a ritual pose. "Hear my words as the words of the gods. Listen and obey him as you would have me, and should the Greater Ones." In intoning the ritualistic words, Odine had, at that moment, divested himself of his rank. After saying this, Odine handed over, in full sight of all, his staff of office, and a weighty torc I had never before seen him wear. I could only assume it was another token of his power.

From people's remarks I could hear, I gathered my assessment was correct. In addition, however, the torc had been a gift to him from King Leeife, and some wondered why he passed it on. A glance back and upward showed the Leeife seemed to have no objection, and indeed appeared to think this all normal and proper. I guessed Odine had warned the king of his actions and the reasons behind it.

The new Chief Skaald took Odine's old place behind King Leeife's throne, and Odine came to stand behind Alaric instead.

Just as he took up his place, there was a stir at the back of the hall, and who should come striding up to the throne without a by-your-leave but the ambassador to the court from Formorrdia.

Although this person did not give me the chills as Bordinn had, he was still a Formorrid and still very strange looking. Like Bordinn, he was reptilian looking, but his eyes were not, at least, as cold and unfeeling as had been Bordinn's. Nor did my Lifestone react to him as it had the Dun Master. I had met this ambassador a few times, and while he did acknowledge me, it was obvious he was uncomfortable in my presence, just as I was in his.

This day he was dressed all in blood red, unusual for him, as he preferred purple usually, and he entered without the slow grace and deliberation that was normal for him.

Reaching the guards who stood just before us, he bowed almost perfunctorily, and was obviously very agitated.

"King Leeife" he began, without even permission from the king, "I come with grave news."

"Speak then, Fordinn, as it seems from your manner you will do so no matter what I say", both ordered and rebuked the king.

"Forgive, Majesty, but this news is dire. My people are upset with your plans to send Prince Alaric with this Eirlandian back to her home. They agree she must leave, but see no reason why the Prince should be put in danger by his accompanying her, as the Eirlandians are sure to be upset by his appearance. We have come to give warning of rumors of war and great unrest in Eirlandian and to not wish to see the prince put in the way of danger."

"This Female," he continued, and his look to me spoke volumes of his disdain, "is quite capable of handling this situation. After all, she has the services of Skaald Odine. We ask, as your allies, to forbid Prince Alaric to go with her; at least until she is settled in her new role and can vouchsafe his journey and health."

Alaric stood, trembling, I assume, with contained anger.

"Emissary Fordinn, while we appreciate the concerns of our allies the Formorrid, I can assure you I will be in no more danger than I would be if I was taking a normal raiding voyage to Eirlandia or anywhere else for that matter."

Alaric turned his eyes to the assembly, who was listening intently to this exchange. "I can assure you, and my people, that I will be no great danger. Tara is my Truwif and I will not be parted from her. She is also Tanista of Kilawey and will most likely be confirmed and crowned High BanRigh of Eirlandia. This brings a great opportunity for all of us.

"The people of Eirlandia are rich in many things that we lack. Proper trade agreements will bring wealth to all of us, not just a few brave warriors. Eirlandia has land to spare, and perhaps in the future a small Vike colony can be established at some sea port for trade and commerce purposes.

"We are both mighty nations but, bonded together by matrimony as well as by treaty and trade, we will become even stronger. Fear not for me, fear is not the emotion of a Vike. Cheer us as we leave and pray for us, if you will, but pray not from fear, but from confidence."

Alaric turned again to Fordinn. "Emissary, tell your High Council that I will go with Tara, and no veiled threat from them will stop me. If we find you have attempted to sabotage this trip, you will find yourselves no longer welcome guests here in Vikland. Do not make us take that step."

Then he sat abruptly and began to speak softly with Skaald Odine, obviously dismissing the emissary without another word.

"Go, now, Emissary Fordinn," said the king. "You have heard Prince Alaric, and he speaks for me in this. The warnings of the Formorrid are heard, but we heed them not. Wish us success, for our success becomes yours. Leave us, now, your message is delivered and reply is given. Wind speed to you."

The Formorrid bowed again and left the chamber with much less speed and much more dignity than he had entered. After he had left, Skaald Odine said softly, "Mark me, we have not heard the last of them. Their enmity towards Eirlandia has never faded, and they will do what they can to bring you harm, Tara, and you also, Alaric. We must be on guard from this moment forward."

Time moved quickly after that, and soon the day of our departure arrived. We were sailing in three large ships, with horses, trade goods, Vike and Eirlandian servants, tons of clothes, jewelry and several large chests of stolen gold, etc. that was being returned to the Eirlandian people. This returned booty would make up much of the royal treasury, at least to begin with.

We had no idea of what sort of state my nation was in, so we prepared for the worst. Seed and farming implements were also being brought, along with experts who would help us determine what needed to be done the quickest and where.

Word had been sent ahead of our departure date and hoped day of arrival. I prayed that Bard Daman had been successful in preparing my people for my return and the sight of the Vike ships. I did not want to cause fear and panic, but hope and relief.

Our leave taking with the king had happened in private the night before. It was a moving time for me as it was obvious that Alaric and Leeife cared deeply for each other and would miss each other greatly. But they were both strong men, and knew that this had to be done for the good of both nations. There is no need to go into details, but it was both a heart warming and heart wrenching farewell.

On the dock I found Vilk, Briggent and Sven waiting for us, along with many others I recognized from the court and Alaric's household. Alaric arrived a short time after I did, along with Skaald Odine and a few of his staff. Formal farewells were given to those watching, then we boarded and were off before I realized it.

My Lifenstone felt warm and comforting against my skin, and I knew the stone was aware we were leaving. Remembering the dream of months past, I wondered when the stone would again speak to me.

The journey was unremarkable and very swift. The weather was perfect, and I couldn't help wondering if Skaald Odine was in any way responsible. I never asked, but watching him one morning as he scanned the skies I saw he made very small gestures with his hands that no one who was not watching him closely would have even noticed.

Upon seeing me, Odine had simply nodded and smiled a somewhat secretive but depreciating smile, as if acknowledging he was, indeed, doing something, but trusting me to make no comment.

Whatever the reason, the winds were favorable and the journey rapid. Sooner than expected there were cries of 'Eirlandia Ho!' from the look outs, and everyone bent swiftly to their tasks of making ready our arrival in my land.

Kilawey is situated inland and is therefore safe from Vike raids. It sits, however, on a large, deep river that allows access to its large port trading facilities. As we traveled up the Dannahu River, I watched from the bow of the Wolfengaard, the ship that had taken me from Eirlandia. Now it was bringing me back home.

As we rounded a wide bend in the Dannahu, I saw the white walls of Kilawey rise up before me. Built on a hill overlooking the wharves, the battlements of Kilawey are reputed to have been made solely by the power of the Sidheran after a battle with the Formorrid.

It was rumored the Siheran had an entrance to their underground world beneath the Royal Enclosure, but no one ever claimed finding the entrance. By human hands or Sidheran, the walls of

Kilawey's Nemed were the most magnificent and awe inspiring in all of Eirlandia.

I had never been to Kilawey, but my father's bard had described the place perfectly and I could recognize many landmarks from his teaching tales.

No flags proclaiming the ArdRigh was in residence flew. Instead, dark purple banners hung lifeless on every pole. It was a sign of mourning, and of royal death. My heart sank as I realized all that had been told to me by Bard Dannan was indeed true. I could only hope that I would be worthy of the challenge laid before me.

Upon arriving at the dock, I noticed a contingent of royal guards and also, so my surprise, Bard Daman, obviously waiting for us. Several saddled, but riderless, mounts were picketed nearby, many more than obviously needed by the guard. I immediately noticed that the tacks on several of the mounts were too fine for use by mere guardsmen.

Alaric, Sven, Odine and Vilk were on the deck with me, I suddenly noticed. Alaric put his hand over mine and smiled encouragingly.

As soon as we were tied up and the plank put down, Bard Dannan started forward. "Hail Tanista Tara, Prince Alaric", he called as he strode toward the ship. "Welcome to Kilawey and also to Eirlandia. Please accept my offer of transportation to the Nemed. I am sure you are weary from travel, and the walk to the Nemed is fairly far on foot."

I stepped forward, as was my right, and answered him formally. "I and my party accept your offer and give our thanks for your welcome, Bard Dannan. Are there wagons available for offloading?"

"Yes, Tanista, all is in readiness. There is another group coming from the Nemed as we speak with wagons and men to help unload your ship. I am sure all will be in place before you are ready to retire for the night."

"All is good then," I replied formally. Then I glanced back to the others behind me. "Bard Dannan," I continued, "may I formally introduce Skaald Odine, official ambassador to the court of Kilawey from King Leeife of the Vikes. Here also is our trusted advisor, Sheifdar Sven, and my guard Vilk, who will continue to be a personal guard here in Kilawey also. You know my mate, Prince Alaric, already."

The Bard made a courtly bow and swept his hand for us to come to land. We disembarked and mounted the steeds swiftly.

The journey to the Nemed was made quickly and without incident. The city was quiet, with few persons milling about, and those we passed appeared to hardly notice us.

We entered through the Gate of the Kings and were hurriedly, I felt, escorted inside; as if Dannan was fearful of our safety. But the Lifestone gave no warning, so I was at ease.

Inside the Greater Hall we were met by those of the Council that could come. Introductions were made and it was decided to send out announcements to all of a Greater Council to be held at the next new moon, seven weeks hence. Alaric was present at these discussions, but quiet through the whole affair, as was Skaald Odine and Sven.

In our rooms, I tried to ask Alaric what he thought, but he put me off saying he did not understand much of the rules and laws that were quoted and that this was my land and my affair.

"As my father rules in Vikland, you rule here" he told me. "I will keep silent, watch, listen and learn as any good hunter does in new territory. I will not put myself forward. Mayhap we can learn more by my silence than my speech."

So saying, he doffed his clothes and sank into a warm tub that had been prepared. I undressed also and joined him, as this was a Royal Chamber, and the baths were very large. What occurred thereafter is not for this telling.

Chapter 13

THERE IS NO REAL need to go into detail about my first few weeks in Eirlandia. It has been well documented in my papers of state, minutes of the council meetings, declarations, etc. Suffice to say that I learned much in very little time and give profound thanks to Bard Daman, ArdDrui Loockan and Skaald Odine for their constant help and advice in matters of which I knew nothing.

Alaric sat by my side, but did not participate in the discussions nor even offer opinions. I believe he won many over by this silence and forbearance, for it was obvious this was not what my courtiers believed would be the case.

Finally, on the new moon, the heads of all the clans of Eirlandia were assembled at Kilawey. Now the business of confirming my claim as the next ruler of all of Eirlandia could begin.

It was the Day of Balance, when the night and day were of equal length. It had been decided that my confirmation would occur at the Harvest Moon, which was only a week or so away.

The announcements had gone out, the Lesser Righs of all the tribes and their Tanists had come and most seemed disposed to allow me to rule. I found out that my exact title would be 'ArdRighian', High Queen. There had never before been an ArdRighian, although some of the tribes had had female rulers before.

That said, the lesser Righs saw in Alaric the Battle Leader they wanted. They respected his strength and his willingness to adhere to our ways, even though he was of the North. Odine was also a great diplomat, and the fact that he and the ArdDrui Loockan had become such fast friends was also helpful to my cause.

The day was waning when Bard Daman entered the Audience Chamber. He wore his cloak of Seven Colors boldly proclaiming his rank as a Chief Bard and came from one of the inner doors so he did not have to walk the length of the hall. In his hand he held the Silver Bough, the branch of bells which mark an announcement of great import for the nation. My heart stood still for a moment when I saw that. It could not bode good things.

"Tanista Tara, Consort Alaric, members of this court and all present, hear me," he called as he approached the dais. He bowed the exact amount that was proper to me and Alaric; then turned and faced the gathering courtiers, warriors and citizens. He rang the bells three times, as was custom when a Great Proclamation was about to be uttered.

"Hear now the words of the Seers. Hear now the words of the Lookouts. Hear now the counsel of the Drui Court. For we come with fearsome news and great sorrow.

"ArdDrui Loockan is dead. Murdered at ritual by an assailant unknown, but believed to be a Formorridd. He was slain not by arrow or sword or knife, but by foul magic. The Drui gathered with him reported a dark cloud coming across the sky and shooting straight down into the center of the Holy Circle and enveloping Loockan, who had no time even to cry out before his body hit the ground, and the cloud dissipated like smoke. The ArdDrui was dead when he fell, according to the healers present. Something had caused his heart to stop and his spirit to immediately flee his body.

It appears our old enemies have emerged once again, and seek to take the heart from us by killing one of our greatest Drui."

Complete, shocked silence reigned for a few moments while I and the rest of the court absorbed this horrible news. Finally, I found my voice.

"What is the counsel of the Drui Court? What other news do we have of this?" I asked.

"Our best Seers were able to track the cloud to a small island off our coast. Scouters went and reported seeing signs of campfires and shelters. From a few items left, it was surmised the people there were Formorrid, probably priests or magicians, or whatever their equivalent is for that race.

"It was decided by the Council that word of this be brought as soon as possible. The Council feels that the confirmation of the Tanista must proceed with all speed, and that she and her Consort be given all powers to lead our nation at this time. There are things known to the Drui Council about her which we will make clear at the Confirmation, but she is unique in her abilities and she brings the might of the Vikes with her, who will be our allies in this, we believe."

At this Odine lifted his staff. "My Rulers, and people of Eirlandia, I speak now as both a High Skaald of the Vikes and also the Vike representative. My king has told me he would support the Eirlandians in any fight they may encounter, including those with the Formorrid. I offer my services and knowledge of the Other Realm along with my Drui brothers in this endeavor."

Pandemonium broke out about then. Everyone started speaking or shouting at the same time. Most seemed inclined to go find the nearest Formorrid and hang them.

I persuaded the hot heads to calm down, reminding them that the actions of a small, possibly independent group did not condemn the whole people. I did not think there were any Formorrid on the island at this time, but I didn't want to be proved wrong.

"Find any Formorrid that might be present among us certainly," I finished. "Bring them here for questioning. But treat them with respect and simply tell them the Tanista wishes to consult with them on some matters pertaining to the relationship between our two peoples."

At this several warriors and a few others left the hall. I imagined the warriors left to gather their people and the others to spread the news. If the Formorrid had spies in my court, they would have heard this and my proclamation, which was what I intended.

"My Righs and High Court members, I suggest we adjourn to private chambers to discuss this more fully," I continued. Standing, I motioned Bard Daman to proceed me, and with Alaric at my side and my other counselors and righs behind, we walked stately from the audience hall into an adjoining chamber where we could discuss the matter before us in private.

Once away from prying eyes and ears, I sent one of the Pagi for food and drink, and had another get candles, so that they would be in place when darkness fell. I did not know how long we would be sequestered, but evening was almost upon us, so we would have need of light soon.

I also sent for a map of Eirlandia and whatever information we had on the whereabouts of the Formorrid. Alaric informed me the Dun we had visited was only a few hours travel from Eirlandia, but that the place was hidden from foes by the Formorrid's magic and would not be found on any of our maps. He was pretty sure he could give an approximate location on a map, however, and he might even be able to get word to his father for Vike troops to attack the Dun should that be necessary. He was fairly certain that, unless the Formorrid had spies and heard Odine's proclamation, the Formorrid would allow the Vikes to land.

While we took a small break from these discussions and illuminations, the Righs came to me in a group, followed by Bard Daman.

"Tanista" said one of the older Righs, "we would like Bard Daman to explain to us your 'special abilities' he mentioned. We would also like to know how you came to even be chosen as Tanista, if you know."

I looked to Bard Daman, who smiled both encouragingly and somewhat secretively, like a cat who knew where the mouse was hiding.

Giving them my attention, I proclaimed, "Gentles, I would know this as much as you would. I was never completely informed as to why the late Ard-Righ had named me Tanista, nor what special gifts or abilities I am supposed to have, as I certainly don't confess to any."

I then directed my gaze at the bard, who was still smiling slightly. "Bard Daman", I addressed him formally, "could you oblige us please? It seems if I am going be confirmed, as the Drui Council advises, it would be best for us all to know exactly why."

Bard Daman bowed his heard and indicated we should sit. He then looked at me and said "Tanista, you must show the Lifestone, which you have wisely kept hidden these many months. It will be proof of what I am about to say."

Struggling not to blush in surprise and consternation that this man knew my secret, I pulled the chain and brought out the piece. The stone was very warm to my touch and almost seemed larger and brighter than I had ever seen it. A faint humming sound seemed to come from it, but no one appeared to notice that except me. At the sight of it, several of the older righs made the Sign of the Fae, in fear or in wonder, I could not decide which.

"This stone, I am told, was my mother's." I told the assembled. "In fact, I have seen my mother through this stone and I know she has taught me many things, but they are things I cannot recall no matter how hard I try. I don't know if the Bard has some way of unlocking my mother's knowledge, but I hope so, as whatever 'gifts' I might have are useless to me as it stands."

Bard Daman bowed his head. "I have not the personal knowledge, but the new ArdDrui does, and he will be here within a day or two at most. What I do have is knowledge of the Tanista's bloodline and the reason she can carry and use a Lifestone. I know that some of you have knowledge of this gem, as I could tell from your reaction. Others of you do not, as you were never taught about them. Some believe them mere legends, but, as you can see, at least one of these survived the Last Great War; and I believe there are more to be found.

"Tanista Tara received this stone from her mother, as she mentioned. What she did not say, because it was not known to Tara, ever, was that her mother was a Sidheran. In fact, her mother,

Marigianna, belonged to the royal line of the Sidheran and was sister to our own late Ard-Righ's Lifemate."

"What the court does not know" Daman continued without a missed beat, "is that the High Consort Mayveer is still alive. She simply withdrew from court life and returned to the Sidheran when it became obvious that her relationship with Brionston would produce no heirs.

"But she knew her sister had had a daughter, and she arranged for a Lifenstone to be given to her niece as both a reminder of her mother and protection against harm.

"It was also a special Lifenstone that carried a hidden message and spell for learning that Tara activated on her voyage to Vikland. The spell was created so that she would have no knowledge of what she was taught until the time was right. That time is now, and the ArdDrui now has knowledge of the spell that will release the Sidheran knowledge and the power Tara now holds."

His words both scared and excited me. What had the Lifenstone taught me that I could not remember? My Aunt was still alive? Would I meet her? Learn from her? How was this secret kept all these years? These thoughts ran through my mind, but I gave no indication of them on my face. I glanced at Alaric, who sat pale and tight lipped. He had known some of this, I knew, about my mother certainly, but not the rest. I wondered if he was angry at me for keeping this secret from him.

My friend and counselor Odine was the first to speak. "Bard Daman, I am sure all of us here have heard news we have not heard before. For some it is completely new, for others some was known and some not. I ask you now, can you tell us the name of the new ArdDrui? Or is that to remain a secret until they arrive?

"And, do you know anything more about the Formorrid threat?"

Chief Bard Daman, bowed his head to Odine and answered him. "As to the name of the new ArdDrui, he is Labraird, a powerful healer and worker of magic. He is one of only a few of the Drui who can read and handle a Lifenstone, as his bloodline also includes Sidheran."

Looking around, he continued; "I know no more of the threat than I announced in open court. It is possible ArdDrui Labraird will know more when he arrives.

"For now, the most important thing we must do is to keep Tanista Tara safe. Also, we must confirm her in her role as ArdRighian with Prince Alaric as her Royal Consort and Battle Lord as soon as possible. We do not need the crowning, just the confirmation with the proclamation to go out to all the tribes. In this way, Tara and Alaric can legally call the tribes together to meet this threat.

"I realize you all have kingdoms to defend, but Tara and Alaric have the whole of the country to be concerned with, not just certain areas. You all know our late Ard-Righ had plans to have Tara brought here and made Tanista before she was captured.

"You have all heard his arguments for this, and you all agreed with his intent. If you had not, Tara would not have been confirmed as Tanista. But she was, so that is now moot. There is no better leader at this time, no one else who has the power, will and knowledge to defeat this threat. And what Tara cannot supply in Battle Leadership, her consort, Prince Alaric, can. I tell you the Great Ones have arranged for this couple to be here in our time of need. Put aside your petty aspirations and unite, or Eirlandia will surely fall to the Formorrid threat, and all we have accomplished will be for naught."

The Righs all looked down, some of them sheepishly, others with a bit of rebellion in their eyes, and still others almost in despair, or maybe hope. None would meet Daman's or my eyes for a few moments. Then, Righ Anluon, the eldest of the provincial kings and the ruler of the Tribe of Loughnass stood up.

"My life and my honor, and that of my tribe do I give this day to our new ArdRighian, Tara of Eirlandia and Sidhera and her consort, Prince Alaric of Vikland," he recited in High Eire, the language of solemn vows. He drew his sword and placed it at my feet.

In keeping with tradition, I took his sword and held it high, then reversed it and brought it point down to the floor before me. I placed my hand gently on its razor-sharp side and pressed just enough to draw a little blood. Then I handed the sword back to him saying, also in High Eire, "Your sword is consecrated with my blood, as your land and people are now consecrated to me. I accept your homage and give you my word to faithfully rule you to the best of my abilities for so long as the people and gods do will it."

After that, one by one, the other Righs pledged their swords and the lives of their tribes to me and each time I repeated the phrase that had come to me, even though I had not known the lines before.

Stealing a glance at Bard Daman, I saw him look at me in amazement, surprise and respect. I suspect he knew I had not known what to say until I said it. I could only assume the Lifestone had given me those words.

After the Official Confirmation was done, we left the Council Chambers, but did not return to the Audience room. Bard Daman went back out to announce that, due to the grave news, court was concluded for the day, but told them that a 'momentous announcement' would be made at the next Nooning of the sun.

Alaric and I adjourned to our quarters and spoke at length with our people there. We told them to be on extra alert and to allow no strangers in, no matter how official they seemed. Vilk was charged with the task of speaking with all unknown people who wished entrance to our chambers.

After Vilk had left, Alaric sat down wearily and motioned me beside him. "So it begins, my love" he said softly. "You must not be afraid, nor worried about the fact you kept your knowledge of the powers of the Lifenstone secret from me. I knew you had Sidheran blood, I suspected you had some sort of special power or sigil. Skaald Odine confirmed it to me not long after we landed in Vikland.

"I only hope this new ArdDrui of yours can help you unlock your power. The Formorrid are strong, ruthless and are said to have terrible weapons of destruction. I would not see this land wasted from their weapons and devices. I think you hold the power to defeat them, but you might need the help of your Sidheran relatives. We must see if your Aunt Mayveer will help you."

"I don't understand any of this" I replied. "What have we done to annoy the Formorrid? Why would they kill our ArdDrui? It makes no sense to me. For generations we have lived apart from each other, each simply avoiding the other. What has changed?"

"I do not really know, my eaglet" he replied. "But I suspect that you are the catalyst for the change. For some reason the Formorrid fear you. That was obvious even at the Dun. They fear you even more now when you are about to become ArdRighian and they don't like the fact that I am with you. I think this combination is what they are really upset about. You and I, we should be enemies, but instead we are husband and wife and we unite the Vike and the Eirlandian. Together, our nations would be formidable in war against any other nation. Perhaps the Formorrid fear we will unite against them."

"By attacking and killing the ArdDrui, they have ensured our response. With you here when this happened, surely they realize that we can call on the Vike to help us in this fight if need be," I replied.

"This just doesn't feel right. I think this is a ploy, but for what I cannot fathom. I think the Formorrid believe that the Vike will side with them, not us, but I don't know why. Or perhaps they hoped this event would demoralize us and send us into panic or despair. If so, they do not understand how we work. No leadership spot is ever left vacant for long, especially if the incumbent is murdered! We must wait and see what they will do next."

I stood and walked to the window. I was much too agitated to sit still. "I think you are right however, and an envoy must be sent to the Sidheran. I will speak to the council on this a little later. I think Bard Daman the best person to send. I only hope the Sidheran will help. I have so much to learn about my mother's people; people I thought were only legends and who had lived long ago but no longer. Obviously, I was mistaken."

"Come here, my love" whispered Alaric. "Come and rest a moment. I fear we will be parted soon, for if there is actual fighting, I must go to lead the troops as Battle Leader. Let us take this time for ourselves and leave the world to its troubles for just a little while."

Nodding, I joined him again, and the world did, indeed, go away for awhile.

Chapter 14

WITHIN A FEW DAYS the new ArdDrui arrived in Kilawey. Labraird looked nothing like the old head of the Drui. He was middle aged, and in the peak of his life. Vitality, strength and power seemed to hover around him, like an almost-visible cloak. His eyes were the most intense green I had ever seen, and I had the uncomfortable feeling that he could read my every thought, if he chose to.

We were meeting in a small chamber deep within the Nemed. The ArdDrui had sent the request for me to come, along with Skaald Odine and Bard Daman, but no one else. "It is not safe, Highness" said his request "for those without magical power or ability to be with us at this time. The power of the Lifestone is formidable, and the spell to unlock it and make available its power to you is even more so. Therefore I entreat the ArdRighian to come with just her two magical advisors."

So here I was, in a small chamber deep within the Nemed. It was obvious from carvings on the walls that this chamber had been used for the working of spells and magic many times before. Invocations to the gods of power and magic were etched on every wall and above the door. There were no windows, of course, but there were symbols even above the small air vents high in the wall that allowed fresh air into the room and allowed smoke from herbs and incense to escape. On the floor was carved a curious design I could not make out. A carving of the Interwoven Ring of Eternity surrounded the inner design.

Power emanated from that spot practically in waves. The Lifestone blazed with life and power, and was warm even through the layers of clothing it rested upon, for I could not have it touching my skin for fear of it burning my flesh.

ArdDrui Labraird lit a small incense burner and walked the room, chanting in a language I could not understand. I assumed he was cleansing and/or blessing the area, however, just from the feel of the room when he was done.

He nodded to Daman and Odine and they gently led me into the circle of power and had me stand, arms outstretched so that they could stand outside the carving but still hold my hands. I wondered why they did this. I would soon have my answer.

The ArdDrui came forward with a staff in his hand. The top of the staff held a large crystal the like I had seen only once before. With a start I realized that the stone on his staff was also a Lifestone.

I had never heard of two of these crystals ever being together. I breathed a silent prayer that Labraird was aware of the potential power of these two items and would take precautions. He extended the staff so that its stone was but inches from mine, and intoned words that, again, I could not understand. Light flared from his stone and struck mine, which flared back. I closed my eyes to the brightness and immediately saw my mother standing before me.

"The time has come", she said. "The Lifenstone's power will be released by the ArdDrui. You will feel some discomfort, daughter, then darkness. When you awake you will have full knowledge of and power over the Lifenstone. And not only this one, but all the others. This is necessary to ensure that no Lifenstone can be stolen by the Formorrid and used against us.

"You will know if a stone is in danger and you will be able to, for all purposes, shut down the stone's power from a distance, rendering it useless to the enemy." She seemed to glide even closer and I felt her hand enclose the stone on my breast. I almost cried a warning about the heat, but she seemed to feel no pain or even discomfort. "Prepare yourself, Daughter" she said.

Then my mind seemed to explode with light and sound and taste and smell and I suddenly realized I could understand the ArdDrui's words as he intoned the spell. What they were did not linger in my mind as my consciousness sought refuge in oblivion, for the power was too much to bear.

Sometime later I awoke in a small but comfortable bed, obviously in a different room. My Lifenstone was cool again, but there was a spark in its heart that had not been there before.

A discreet cough made me turn my head. ArdDrui Labraird was there, holding a cup of something that smelled wonderful and steamed slightly in the air. "Drink, ArdRighian, the herbs will clear your head and give you strength." He ordered.

I obeyed and felt better before the cup was even drained.

I cannot recall precisely all that was said, but he gave me instructions regarding the use and power of the Master Lifestone for what seemed like an eternity.

I know that time passed as meals were sent in and I slept more than once. Although I knew the words to unleash the power of the stone, I needed to understand the constraints of its use as well as the times when it needed to be given free reign.

I also learned about my mother's people and their history and lore. It seemed I was a Child of Prophecy and, as such, was fated to do wonderful things, things that the Sidheran would go to any lengths to see occur and the Formorrid any length to prevent.

I, it seemed, was the crux of this whole incident with the Formorrid. Once they became aware of my existence, which happened when I visited their Dun, they became first concerned then frightened when it became obvious that the Great Forces were bringing about the events of the Prophecy of Doom, as they named it, and the Prophecy of Redemption as the Sidherans named it.

Finally, Labraird pronounced me ready and I was escorted to a small chamber just outside the council room where I bathed and was dressed in the formal robes of state.

For the first time I donned the Cloak of Authority and held the Staff of Power in my hand. I walked through the door no longer Tanista, but ArdRighian of Eirlandia. I had been proclaimed by the Council and now I was ready to take my place as ruler of my country.

Alaric met me on the other side of door and offered his arm as escort. Together we traveled the length of the hall, which was crowded with representatives of every clan, trade and Drui branch; come to pay their respects and give their oaths to the new Ard Righian.

For the first time I saw and sat upon the High Throne, which had not been present in the Royal Hall before this. It was the custom to remove the Throne iif there was no Ard, Righ or Righian. This had happened only a handful of times in our history, usually when the Tanist or Tanista was not of age and a Regent ruled in their place.

As before with the Righs in Council Chambers, the heads of the Greater Families and the various Guilds and the Armed Forces came forward to give their oaths of Fealty and to receive mine in turn. The Drui Class, of course, had already given theirs through the old ArdDrui. But ArdDrui Labraird came forward to personally give his oath, and the heads of the various types of FighDrui, from teachers, bards, healers, seers, scholars, etc. also came forward on behalf of their individual disciplines.

The ceremony was long and somewhat tedious, but somehow I was not tired even at the end of it. It was as if I was being constantly fed more strength and ability to endure as time passed, and I realized the Lifenstone was making its presence felt fully for the first time in my life.

At long last the oaths were given and received and the last of the Drui gave their blessing upon my reign and the land in general. We went to the banquet hall for a meal and I learned that the Formorrid had been tracked to an island just outside our borders. For now, there was nothing we could do. The murderers had escaped temporarily. However, word had come from King Leeife that Vike warships were on their way and would arrive at the island within a few days.

Chapter 15

WITHIN A FEW DAYS of the crowning, word came that the Vike warships had arrived at the Formorrid's home island and surrounded it, laying siege to those inside.

However, the Formorrid were not without weapons and power, and they had been bombarding the ships with large spheres of lead, and a few of the ships had been damaged. So far, no magical devices had been employed, but the Vikes were sure it was only a matter of time.

Word also came of the location of a group of Formorrid mages holed up in a cave near the western coast of Eirlandia. The area around the cave was filled with magical wards, and the scouts could not get close. However, some of our Far Seers reported what seemed to be a military build up in the area, which was being screened magically. With this news, Alaric began to take command of our forces, as was his right and duty as Battle Leader. He sent out scouts, accompanied by such Fighdrui as were trained in Far Seeing and also in protective magic.

Then he began ordering the nation's forces, having those Righs who were closest gather their troops to meet him at the rendezvous place a short distance from the magical border of the Formorrid's camp. He then sent word out to all the other tribes to prepare their troops and await his summons. He would arrange a large band of defenses so that the Formorrid would have to fight their way across the whole land and all his forces before reaching Kilawey.

"If we cannot stop them", he told me one evening, "we can at least delay and harrow them. We can hopefully weaken them so that the Royal forces here can finish them off."

Within half a moon of my crowning, my Battle Leader consort marched out with a large contingent of both soldiers and drui. The Nemed was much quieter after they left, with many of the Royal FighDrui contingent gone with Alaric.

ArdDrui Labraird was, of course, still here, along with Skaald Odine and several other older, wiser and very powerful Drui magic workers. For several days I studied and learned from both Labraird and Odine. I found that I could use both Vike and Eirlandian magic with help of the Lifenstone.

Word had been sent to the Sidheran asking aid, and we were waiting to hear their response before I, too, would go out to face the Formorrid. This was my fate, and the war could not be won without my presence. This Labraird had made very clear.

"You are the Chosen One" he had told me more than once. "Your Lifenstone is the strongest one the Sidherans ever produced. It is the Master Stone over all the others, as I have explained. With it you command the elements themselves, within reason. The stone is linked to you, now, and no other can use it. This is both good and bad, for while it means it cannot be used by the Formorrid it also means than no one else can use it in your stead or if you die, at least not in time to do anything of worth."

I looked at him questioningly, and he explained his statement more fully. "While the stone can be re-keyed, it takes time and a Master Mage of the Sidheran to do it. I doubt very much one of their Masters will be on the battle field, even if some of the lesser mages and some of their soldiers are present."

I listened and absorbed all I could. Then I practiced spells and learned to weave the power the Lifestone gave me. About a tenight after Alaric left, word came that the Sidheran had agreed to help us. Indeed, it was no less personage than Mayveer herself who came with the news, and with counsel of her own.

I was holding court as usual. War or no, the kingdom had to be ruled. I had formed a Royal Council to rule in my stead once I left for the field, but until then there were many things that needed my decision. I had just finished giving judgment on a matter of interpretation of the law between two rival tribes when the doors to the chambers suddenly became shrouded in a thick mist that glowed much as my Lifestone did when in use. The guards attempted to move into the midst, but found they could not move.

"Sidheran", commented Labraird somewhat dryly. "They rarely bother with doors these days." Indeed, even as he spoke, the mist cleared and a tall, light-skinned, white haired, beautiful woman stood just inside the chamber.

A gasp went up from those in attendance, for the woman was at once recognized. "Principea Mayveer", breathed Daman, half in disbelief and half in almost worshipful tones.

The woman looked around, smiled at a few of the courtiers, then walked, nay, almost floated, to just before the throne. She bowed, as one equal to another. There was nothing of deference about her stance, but she was also respectful and held herself in confidence but not arrogance.

"ArdRighian Tara of Eirlandia," she began, her voice mellow, but with obvious carrying power. "I bring you greetings from your allies the Sidheran. The High Council has seen the Ancient Enemy again emerge and we stand ready to help you defend Eirlandia, which is as much our home as yours. The Mages of the Sidheran are massing as we speak, and all of the Lifenstones are in tune with yours. As I am related to you by blood, I shall act as temporary liaison between you and the Sidheran forces, as I am much more use to communicating long distance by thought than you are." The last sentence was said softly, and I know only I and the closest advisors heard her.

Her words told me that I had something more to learn, as transmittal of thought between people had never been taught to me. A glance to Labraird confirmed that he had not known of this ability, and I wondered if it was inherent in the Sidheran or the Lifenstone.

"Welcome, Principea Mayveer," I answered formally and with enough volume to carry. "I am pleased to make the acquaintance of my mother's sister. Your aid I gladly welcome and that of your countrymen. I am sure you can teach me much, for I am not used to magic and must learn much quickly."

"I am honored, ArdRighian, and stand ready to help, as do all Sidheran," she answered formally.

I stood then, at some inner urging I did not truly understand. "Come, Aunt Mayveer, let us retire. The audience is done for the day in any event, which I am sure you knew and so timed your arrival accordingly. We have much to discuss and little time in which to do it."

So saying I descended the throne and Mayveer, myself, Odine, Daman, Labraird and my ever-present guard Vilk, walked through the now silent hall and into the smaller council chamber beyond.

Once in the council chamber, I sent Vilk for refreshments. We settled down at the round table in the center of the room. Mayveer produced a map of Eirlandia and the surrounding islands seemingly from out of the air.

I raised my eyebrow but made no comment. Stories of the abilities of the Sidheran had told of their ability to move things and even people from place to place. It was not even considered a notable feat among them. Mayveer spread out the map and showed us the exact locations of the Formorrid. She also pointed out a gold circle near one of the large Formorrid encampments which I had never seen on any other map or chart.

"This circle marks an entrance to Sidhera," she said. "The Formorrid are not aware of it, but if they become aware then they could possibly breach the entrance and gain admittance to our kingdom. We cannot allow this to happen, and you Eirlandians cannot allow it either. We Sidherans are relatively small in number; we cannot afford to lose a single life. Besides that, the knowledge and weapons the Formorrid would gain is beyond words of warning."

She looked at me then, her eyes calm yet full of both hope and despair. "Tara, this is where you must make your stand. You must defeat the Formorrid who encamp so near our entrance. These are the ones who killed your old ArdDrui and these are the ones most skilled in magic and the most knowledgeable.

"We are certain the Formorrid suspect an entrance to Sidhera near their camp and that is why they choose here. Otherwise there is no rhyme or reason to their choice as the area has no strategic value otherwise."

I looked around at the others. Odine, Daman and Labraird all nodded. "The Sidheran Tuath must be protected at all costs" Labraird proclaimed. "There is too much at stake. The fate of Sidhera is the fate of Eirlandia. So it was told to the first Drui, Ammerigian, when first the Sons of Eirl came to these shores and bargained with the Sidheran for settlement rights. Our fates are intertwined."

"Even among my people," interjected Odine, "stories of the history of Sidhera and Eirlandia have always recounted the strange and mystical bond between the two peoples.

"Many believe that the two clans are actually related, far back in history, and that only together are they powerful enough to overcome our mutual enemy, the Formorrid. There are vague writings in our scrolls that speak of this time, when Vike, Eirlandian and Sidheran will unite and fight a single common enemy. Many of my brethren discount these writings, but I understand now that this battle is, indeed, the one referred to.

"The Dark Tribe grows too strong, both in magic and in military strength. If they defeat the Eirlandians and the Sidheran, then I am sure Vikland would next come under their rule. My people have no wish to be slaves to the Dark Tribe."

"ArdRighian," Labraird spoke the title formally, "all the Drui stand ready to help. The very birds of the air and beasts of the field and forest will come forth to help defend this land. You are the Sovereign, the Spirit of the Land made manifest in flesh. Command the Drui and they will tell the land and all its inhabitants, mortal, animal, plant and even elemental what they must do. The Formorrid do not understand this about us. They believe in no greater Power, no Source of strength and courage and wisdom beyond themselves. We, however, know how to draw upon the Great River of Knowledge and Strength. Together we can and will defeat them."

"Then let it be so", I answered quietly. "Make ready all that needs to be. We leave at the rising of the Reborn Moon."

At that moment Vilk arrived back with a group of servants bringing water, mead, ale, cakes and fruit.

Vilk took one look at me and said, "If you leave without me, Alaric will have my head when he finds out. I do not wish to be headless. I am coming with you."

"Of course you are," I answered almost laughingly, for the look on his face was so comical that it could not help but lighten the mood. This was obviously his intention, for he grinned, winked and went to stand behind me, as always.

Chapter 16

THE AREA WHERE WE camped was breathtaking to behold. The mountains were at our back and the large Plain of Mungreat stretched out before us, as far as eye could see. We were in the foothills of the Winckenlaw Mountains, and the forests here were lush and almost virginal.

Not far away we could see the smoke rising from the Formorrid's encampment, but the rise of the hills and the forest, along with the magic of the Drui, kept us from being seen.

Two days after we camped, Alaric arrived, having gone around the Formorrid's camp in order to remain undetected. One look and I knew he had successfully routed the other encampment.

"The Formorrid are gone", he told me as he drank some mead after changing from his traveling clothes. "The ones on the island are all dead, according to the reports received from my father's forces.

"The mages in the other camp are gone. We don't know if they are dead or simply gone, since we never got a count of how many were actually at the cave. We have bodies, but no way to know who they were.

"Perhaps the Sidheran can help there. All we know is that no one and nothing is left. If they had devices or machines they are gone also. It is as if no one was there, except for the dead bodies, and we don't know how they even died. Many have no wounds on them. I have never seen the like. The Vikes do not fight with magic, we fight with sword and spear and the occasional bow." His eyes were haunted and I imagined he had witnessed things he had never encountered before and trying to digest the sights.

"Well, the main thing is they are gone, at least from there," I answered. "We will be launching an attack against their camp within a day or so. The Drui and the Sidheran mages are meeting right now to decide on the date and time.

"I do not understand it all", I admitted. "It has something to do with the positions of the sun and moon and the advice of the Greater Elementals. Labraird, Odine, Daman and Mayveer are all there. They seem to know what is going on. They will tell me and I will simply go where they want when they want. I get the feeling that it is not I who am important, in and of myself, but my role as Bearer of the Key Lifestone. The only thing I know is that your presence is also important, as the 'male and female representatives of the Land must be present', according to Labraird and Daman."

"Drui and Skaalds," laughed Alaric, "they are all alike. They think in symbols, not in concrete things. Well, they are the learned ones here. I am simply happy to be back with you, no matter what the morrow may hold." So saying he put down his cup and reached for my hand. "We live in perilous times, my love. But I have faith in both our people and in the Sidherans. We will prevail, and when the Formorrid threat is through, we will make of this land a glorious thing, the envy of all the world."

I laughed nervously. "Let us hope not too glorious, I don't want another empire deciding to attempt to conquer us because we have too much. I will be happy with our nations at peace and living in prosperity, hope and honor."

What more that might have been said was stilled as the tent flap opened, and my chief advisors entered.

"Tomorrow at Dawning" proclaimed Labraird as he strode in. "We will use the power of Light to overcome the Dark Tribe. The spirits of Air, Water and Land are also with us. The Formorrid will find themselves fighting their worst fear, Elemental Light and Fire."

Labraird grinned, obviously pleased with himself. I felt somewhat bewildered as I had no real idea of what he was talking about. My face must have shown this, since Mayveer's laugh tinkled in the air.

"Labraird, hold your speech. Our poor ArdRighian has no idea of what you speak." Then she sobered. "Worry not, niece. All will be made clear to you tomorrow. Odine and Daman will put you through some meditation tonight before retiring. In the morning you will know what to do. Trust in the Lifenstone, and do as your inner self prompts and all will be well."

I nodded and gestured for them to be seated and eat. Tomorrow was going to be, I knew, a long, tiring and eventful day. I did not know then how right I would be.

The Bard and Skaald did, indeed, guide me through some meditations that night before I slept. But I cannot recall what they were. I remember hearing singing, in both Vike and Eirlandian, and also Eirl as I lay, eyes closed, in a small hut away from the noise of the camp.

I knew Vilk stood guard outside, along with Alaric and several others. Labraird and Mayveer were off together somewhere. I had a feeling they were putting together the final touches on the attack.

The next morning I awoke to darkness, but knew that dawn was not far off, for a small amount of light brightened beyond the tent opening. I thought this fact somehow strange, but quickly put it out of my mind as Alaric stirred beside me and opened his eyes.

"Blessings on you today" he said in Vike. It was the traditional words spoken before a band left for adventure or trading or war. "May the Forces find you favorable."

"May the Sword of Mourruiagan guard your back", I answered in Eirlandian. This was our saying to our soldiers and sailors when they went to battle.

Vilk came in just then with hot drinks and barley cakes. "You will need to eat, ArdRighian," he said with a grin. "The Bard Daman bid me tell you to make sure to drink all of the tea, as it has special herbs to give you strength and to open you to the greater Force. Whatever that might mean."

He smiled and I smiled back. Vilk was not only my personal guard, but also a friend.

"Do not worry, I will eat and drink my fill, as I know not when I will be able to do so again." I answered.

After breaking our fast, Alaric stepped outside to have a final word with the counselors. I donned the special robe that Daman had left for me. It was white, with silver embroidery of designs I did not recognize but which I instinctive knew were symbols of protection and power. Daman had said this was of Sidheran make and design and would protect me from both the spells of the Formorrid and any backlash of my own power from the Lifenstone.

Indeed, the stone was already warm, and as instructed I took it from my neck and slipped it off its chain. Next to the chest on which the robe had lain was a wooden staff made of oak, the strongest and most magical of all the plants. Silver wire had been wrapped around the top to secure a small gem holder. Carefully, I placed the Lifenstone and its holder into the opening at the top of the staff, then pulled up the wire to secure it in place.

Holding my right hand before the stone I spoke the Words of Securing that Daman had taught me. The Lifenstone blazed for a moment, and when the light dimmed, I saw that it seemed to have fused itself in place. Now, no matter what happened, the stone would not come loose from the staff until I spoke the Words of Unbinding.

The ground was somewhat cool to my feet, but I had been told I could wear no covering. I had to have contact with the earth.

I walked out of the tent in time to see Sven and several other men head out of camp. I knew that they were going to sneak around to the far end of the Formorrid camp in order to pick off any who fled.

There were several Eirlandian mages with them, I knew, as well as Fighdrui who had fighting magic powers. Others would tend to the sides of the encampment.

The Formorrid would be surrounded, although the fog I now saw shrouding the valley and Formorrid encampment would hide that fact until it was too late. I suddenly realized that the fog was some weather magic put in place by those Drui with power over weather. I also understood that the fog would vanish the moment we were ready to attack so that the Sacred Fire would burn that much brighter upon our foes.

I spotted Alaric, Labraird, Odine and Mayveer, and walked toward them, the ever-watchful Vilk a few steps behind. Reaching the group, I nodded as Labraird pointed to a hill slightly before and to the right of us, which was bare of trees and would look down almost directly on the Formorrid encampment.

"We will attack from there," he stated. "The four of us will set up the protective barrier. You will stand in the middle and direct the Sacred Fire through the Lifenstone. Strike for the tents first, to make sure there are no hiding places. Then call the Greater Lightning to strike the leaders. You need not know who they are, their magic will attract the lightning to them. Once the leaders are dead, we will ask for surrender. If they do not, we will have to destroy them all. We will help you with the lesser Formorrid, but only you will be strong enough to break through their magical barrier to attack first the tents then the leaders."

Odine looked at me seriously. "Do not assume this will be easy" he said. "They will fight back. We don't know what kinds of weapons or magic they may have, but your Lifenstone is linked to all the others, and the combined strength will be enough to destroy what must be destroyed. You will use the staff to direct the Power. Choose your targets carefully. We do not wish to damage the land any more than necessary."

I nodded, my throat going dry. It was one thing to talk about this in the privacy of your rooms or even in your tent, but out here, in the dim light of pre-dawn, the enormity of what I was about to attempt came crashing in on me.

Daman took my hand, apparently realizing my nervousness and thoughts. "Do not dwell on this, Tara," he counseled gently. "You will be but the channel through which the energy flows. The Great Ones will direct you and you will have no cause for shame in your actions. You will do great deeds today that will be sung for generations to come, and the people will hail you as savior and deliverer as well as their rightful sovereign. Through you the land will become stronger and Eirlandia will enter into a time of peace and prosperity such as it has never known. The High Powers have decreed this, they will cause it to happen, do not fear."

Then he handed me another cup. "Drink", he commanded. "It is water from the Sacred Well of Liffey. This drink is all the beverage you may have until your work is done, but the waters of the well are magical and healing and will give you strength unlike any other drink or food." I took the cup and drained it, feeling better afterwards.

"Come," said Mayveer then, reaching for my hand. "Ride with me. My steed is strong and can carry us both. We must reach the hill just before sun rise, so we cannot walk."

Mayveer's steed was indeed strong, having the look of a warsteed, not a lady's mount. But he was gentle and allowed me to mount without an issue. There was no saddle, just a type of blanket with straps. The reins were only to help you hold on, I noticed, and did not actually guide the steed.

Mayveer saw my expression and laughed gently. "Our horses are not like yours,' she said. "They are intelligent and understand our wants and needs without restrains or devices. Finnias knows where we need to to, how to get there, and to accomplish this in the quickest way. Hold to me, I will hold to him, he will not let us fall, no matter what."

So saying, she said a word a Sidheran and we started off, the steed indeed moving quickly through the wood and over streams. We arrived at our destination much sooner than our horses would have, even if the rider had known the area well.

The hilltop was dotted with small stones that had ancient carvings upon them. I recognized the old symbols for many of our deities, and also the symbols for power, strength and storm. The Lifestone on my staff seemed to almost shimmer. It was not shining brightly, but had, instead, a sort of nimbus around it, that pulsed with a gentle light.

Mayveer bid me dismount and, after doing so herself, gave another word of command to Finnias, who took itself off down the hill.

"He will wait for us in safety," she informed me. "I do not wish to put any innocent creature in peril with what we do here." Nodding in agreement, I looked around for a place to stand where I could see the encampment the best. It was hard to know since below was still fog and mist, although I could hear the sound of many bodies and animals and the strange sounds I assume were machinery of some sort.

"They bring The Eye of Ballor" Mayveer said, with a slight tremble in her voice. "This is a terrible machine of destruction. You will have to attempt to destroy the operators of this device before all else, so that they cannot bring the machine to bear on us, our camp, or the entrance to the Sidhe."

She pointed to a group of stones at the crown of the hill. "There is the spot you must stand, it offers the best protection. There is a stone you can place the staff into that will allow you to move the staff as you wish, but you won't have to actually keep it upright yourself. You will need to hold it, of course, but the stone will help keep the staff in place should they try to capture the Lifenstone with magic. There are also stones to lean upon and even sit if needed."

Nodding, I wound my way around the other standing stones until I reached the spot she had pointed to. The stones formed a small semicircle, with the staff stone she described within the center of the space a few other stones of various sizes around it. The ground was soft with grass and moss on my feet, and almost felt warm. I would not get a chill doing this, which had been a concern of mine.

I placed the staff into the obvious hole designed for it and closed my eyes. In my mind's eye I brought up the image of Tarantitas, the god of Lighting and Keeper of the Sacred Fire. "Tarantitas, hear me", I whispered in the old tongue of Eirl. "Keeper of the Sacred Fire, light your hearth and send your torch. I, Tara, wielder of the Master Lifenstone, call to you.

Come to the aid of your people. Burn off the fog so that we may strike."

An intake of breath from Mayveer, who stood just outside the entrance to the circle, made me open my eyes.

The fog was swiftly dissipating, and shafts of lighting were lacing down from a cloudless sky on to the camp below. The Formorrid were running every which way, trying to ascertain what had happened and why, I am sure. I saw a few look up my way and point. The shadows hid me from their normal sight, but I knew that magic would be able to pierce the shadows of the stones and tell them that there was someone up here.

Scanning below, I saw a large object in the middle of camp. It was like nothing I had ever seen, but my heart pounded in fear at the very sight of it. I knew that this strange device, which seemed made of black stone and wheels and a strange metal I could not identify, was the Eye of Ballor, the terrible machine of which Mayveer had spoken. I narrowed my eyes, willing my sight to tell me who of those below were the workers of this device. I pointed the Lifestone in the direction of the machine, and waited a moment.

Suddenly five figures in black robes came running from a nearby tent. They began to work on the device, and the noise of turning wheels came up to me clearly. Here were my targets, and I wasted no time. "Send the Lighting of Justice upon them", I commanded in Eirl and bade the Master Lifestone do my bidding.

An intense light flared out from the Lifenstone, a beam so bright that I shielded my eyes for a moment until a type of haze dimned the beam so I could watch. The beam came down and then divided, through what property of magic I do not know, into separate beams that simultaneously stroke the five figures, bathing them in the light. There was no sound, but as quickly as it struck, the beam shut off, and the smoldering remains of the five Formorrid were all that was left.

I could not look, and shifted my gaze instead to the tents, which were my next targets. Again I commanded the Lifenstone to life, and it obeyed me. Soon the camp was filled with fires, and the Formorrid in the tents ran out, some themselves in flames that would not be extinquished.

With the camp ablaze I stopped to rest. Mayveer brought me more water, which both slaked my thirst and bolstered my spirits. Suddenly a loud noise boomed from the camp and we looked to see that someone had activated the Eye.

Mayveer cried out and crouched down, her hands over her head. I shouted something I do not even recall, and the staff blazed with light, creating a shield over both of us. The black cloud the Eye had sent out hit the shield, but did not penetrate.

I could hear the screams of rage from those below. Obviously they had never encountered anything that could deflect the Eye before. I smiled grimly and sighted their camp once more. "Lighting of Justice, destroy this machine of destruction. And seek and destroy the leaders of this host." I commanded the Lifenstone. Light again poured out of the stone and engulfed the Eye of Balor and struck several figures in the camp. But although the Formorrid died, the machine did not appear destroyed or even damaged.

A large figure dressed in red, whom I had not seen before, appeared from behind the machine. He carried a large staff also, with a pure black crystal mounted at its top. He pointed it upwards in my direction.

"Hear me, you at the top" I heard him clearly say. "You cannot destroy this machine nor the whole of the Formorrid contingent. One Lifenstone is not powerful enough, no matter what your people may have told you. Surrender the false ArdRighian, Tara, to us, and we will leave your island in peace. We do not quarrel with the Eirlandian people, or the Vikes, or even the Sidheran, whom we know you have called upon for assistance. We wish only Tara, and we even swear we will not harm her. But she must not be allowed to rule, for if she does then we as a nation are in jeopardy and we will not sit by idly and see our people perish."

My heart was in my mouth. Why would the Formorrid want me so badly? Then I remembered what Daman and the others had said. I was The Child of Prophecy. My reign, with Alaric by my side, was to be the start of the decline of the Formorrid. I was glad it was I who heard the mage, so I could be certain of his exact words. 'One Lifenstone is not powerful enough' he had said. Very well, then, I would just have to have more than one Lifestone.

Consentrating on the unfamiliar words I had memorized that would link the Lesser Lifestones to me, I called upon the Greater Ones and the Powers of Earth, Air, Fire and Water to speed to me the powers of all the other Lifestones within the three sacred realms, thereby assuring that every Lifestone, no matter where its location, would be linked in power to mine. I cannot say how I knew it had been accomplished, but after a few minutes, I felt a strange sensation I had never felt before, and knew that the Lifestones were now, indeed, all joined together.

I willed my voice to carry and cried out these words. "Hear me, Formorrid. It is I, the ArdRighian of Eirlandia who speaks. I thank you for your words regarding the Eye of Balor and I have taken them to heart. My people will not give me up, not for all the promises in this world and next. Instead, we give you the chance to withdraw, on the condition that you never again attempt to interfere with the ruling of this land, or any other. Withdraw now, and send your emissary to Kilawey to sue for peace, and I will not bring all the power to bear upon you which is mine to bring."

"Foolish girl", the Formodian answered. "You will rue the day you ever left Vikland. I never trusted you when you were at my Dun, and I trust you less even now."

And it was then I realized that I bandied words with none other than the Formorrid Emmissary

Bormid, in whose Dun I had resided briefly between my capture in Eirlandia and my voyage to Vike.

I remembered how Alaric had said he never wanted me there, and how he tried to find out things about me just before we left for Vikland. I knew he was a great mage, having seen the strange and wonderous devices on his island. I wondered if he was the designer and creator of the Eye of Balor, and how many other terrible devices he had created and intended to use against us.

"You cannot hope to win this battle" he continued. "Even now your forces are being defeated. It will be but a matter of time before your Council will be begging us for terms, not the other way around. Prepare to meet your High Ones, Tara of Eirlandia!"

He turned away, then, and walked back behind the machine. I heard the sound of its power and quickly called up the Lightning one more time. This time, however, I poured into the bolt all the power of all the Lifenstones of Eirlandia and, I suspected, Sidhera as well. As the bolt lept from the staff, I screamed, for I felt as if the power of the Divine Lighting was coursing through me as well as the staff and the Stone at its head. It was not until several hours later than I learned I was correct in my feeling.

Chapter 17

I AWOKE BACK AT OUR camp. The Lifenstone again lay in its setting on my chest. I felt drained, yet curiously whole and at ease. I turned my head, and saw Alaric sitting a small way aways, looking over a map. His body lines told me he was tired, but satisfied. "We must have won", I said softly.

At the sound of my voice, Alaric looked over at me and smiled. "Indeed we did," he answered. "A near rout, I would say. All that remains of the Eye of Balor, Emmissary Bormid, and his team can be carried away by a small horsecart. As for the other troops? I would be surprised if the clean-up crew finds anything left to do."

He walked over and took a sit where he could hold me hand. "We have won a great victory, and our loses were small. But I am told that a great challenge still awaits us. Well, awaits you, actually."

My eyebrow quirked at this. "What great challenge?" I asked. "I have yet to fully take up ruling. What more is there to do that I don't already know about?"

"You must create anew the Ruling Crowns of Eirlandia," Labraird answered as he entered the tent. I looked askance at him. Had he heard my question, or was it just strange timing on his part. I knew I would never have the answer to that question.

"In ages long past, the Ard-Righ or Righian and their consort wore special crowns with powers to keep the land united and the threat of the Formorrid and the Vikes at bay," he continued. "Obviously, the Vikes are no longer a threat and are, indeed, our allies. The crowns would ensure their loyalty and would secure Eirlandia against any future dealings with the Formorrid or other nations of which we presently have no knowledge, but who might one day be a threat.

"The old crowns were lost or destroyed," he continued as he took a seat near Alaric, "no one knows which, in one of the last battles of the last Formorrid Conflict. The Sidheran mages have indicated they stand ready to help create new crowns, as does Skaald Odine and, of course, the drui that have this sort of knowledge.

Even as we speak, the materials are being gathered and prepared. But the power of the Lifestones will be needed to complete the work. The sooner we can complete the crowns, the sooner we can breathe easier as a people, knowing our future is secured."

"I am strong enough to travel," I replied, and sat up to prove it. "When can we leave?"

Alaric looked askance at me, and Labraird glowed. Just then the door opened yet again and

Skaald Odine entered. "Ah, Tara, I see you have recovered. And from the look on Labraird's face I would say you have learned of the new task and wish to get started on it as soon as possible."

I nodded. "I am well. I wish this done so we can get on with our lives."

"Indeed," he agreed. "Spoken as a true leader. It is late now, but we can leave in the morning. The Sidherans have agreed to let you travel, by closed litter, through their kingdom back to Kilawey. It is safer and a much easier journey. Once there, the good mages, the drui, and myself will finish the work on the crowns and determine the best date for their infusion with the Lifestone power. Do not worry, all will be done soon."

"Let us hope so, Skaald," Alaric answered. "I am not used to all the magic. Give me a foe that fights with bow and spear and axe, and I shall be there. But ones who use strange machines, and magics beyond my reckoning, well, that is another matter."

And so we spent one more night at camp; then I and Alaric traveled by litter through the Realm of the Sidheran.

There is naught to write of this journey as the litter was closed in, and we heard no sounds as we traveled, not even that of the horses or men who accompanied us. After a length of time that I cannot state, we came out again into sunlight, and the door of the litter was opened.

Before us, just down a small slope, lay Kilawey. Ordering the windows unshuttered, we passed the group of Sidherans who had led us through their country and entered swiftly the Royal Nemed.

At the Night of the Moon's Fullness, Labraird, Odine and Daman again entered the royal court and bade me change into a gown of white and accompany them, along with Alaric, to the Sacred Grove.

Upon arrival, I saw fourteen cowled figures, each one a color that stood for one of the Tribes of Eirlandia, along with empty places for Odine as the representative of Vike, Daman as representative of the Bards, and for myself and Alaric. A large white stone stood in the center of the circle of people and upon it were two covered forms, which I assumed were the crowns.

Labraird went to the east side of the stone and gestured for us to stand on the west side. My Lifestone began to warm and I quickly brought it out so that it rested upon my clothes. Labraird smiled slightly in what seemed to be satisfaction, then faced both Alaric and I, with a far away look in his eyes, as if he saw something just above and behind us that neither of us could see.

"I summon the Greater Ones, the Protectors, the Spirits of the Ancestors of this land, Eirlandia," he began in High Eirl, the language of magic and antiquity. "I invoke the Three-Fold Way, and the Five-Fold Treasures of Life. For the love of this land, for its safety and continuance, we give both thanks and ask for blessing. Set your power, Oh Mighty Ones, into these tokens of Rule. May these crowns ensure the lasting peace and prosperity of Eirlandia and her allies."

He took off the cloth that had hidden the crowns. I remember I gasped slightly in wonder. Made of a material I was later to learn was almanite, the crowns were decorated with small gems of varying kinds, with a Lifenstone placed high and center in the more elaborate of the crowns, and a smaller Lifenstone in the plainer crown.

I understood which crown was for whom then; the larger crown being for the actual Ard Righ or Riaghian, and the smaller, less elaborate crown for the consort.

Their cunning design made them adjustable to the size of the person wearing it. These crowns would never be too small or too large, they would never require adjustment to them in any way. They were works of wonder and of such craftsmanship as I had never before seen.

"ArdRighian Tara of Eirlandia" intoned Labraird formally, "take your Lifenstone and place it on top of the Lifenstone that is on your crown." I followed his instructions and placed the two stones facing each other.

"Now concentrate on your stone and will its power to flow into and be shared by this new Lifenstone," he commanded.

I closed my eyes, and saw the two stones before me. "Heed my words", I said silently in Eirl to my old Lifenstone. "Share your power, stone of my mother and her people. Link yourself to it as you are linked with all the others of your ilk. Share your power, but be not diminished."

I felt my command take hold and a feeling of power washed over me and went to the crown. A moment later the power returned to me, feeling different yet whole and strengthened.

"It is done," decreed Labraird. I opened my eyes, and saw that the Lifenstone in the crown now also glowed, as did my own. "Take the Master Lifenstone, Tara, and place it upon the consort's crown." Labraird ordered. "It too must be linked. It bears a much smaller stone, and less powerful, but it is not without power itself, for in some times the Consort must rule and have the power to protect the land in the place of the Ard-Righ or Righian."

I did as commanded and placed the Lifenstone at the top of the crown. This time it was Labraird who commanded the stone, and in a language I did not know. Again the Lifenstone blazed, and the consort's crown sparkled in a dazzling display of light. In a few moments all was again quiet.

I glanced over at Alaric, who was eyeing the crown with a mixture of speculation and reluctance. Without command, I retrieved my Lifenstone and placed it around my neck once more, letting it stay in full view.

"The Blessings of the Northern Ones be upon these crowns and those who wear them," proclaimed Odine into the silence. "Ever shall Vikland be a friend to Eirlandia, as long as the rightful rulers wear these crowns."

Each person in the circle also gave their blessings in the name of the tribe or group they represented. At the end of it, Labraird came around to our side of the altar and gestured us to step back a bit. Upon impulse, I got down on one knee. Somehow I knew what was going to happen next, although I had not anticipated this when I had come in.

Labraird lifted first the Consort Crown and turned to Alaric, who hastily followed my example when he realized what was about to happen.

"Do you swear, Prince Alaric of Vikland, consort of Tara, High Queen of Eirlandia, to faithfully perform your duties of Consort for the protection and preservation of this land, before all others?" Asked Labraird in a ringing voice, one meant to carry to all three worlds, I believed.

"I so swear," answered Alaric. "As I love your High Queen, so do I love this land; and I swear to protect both of them for as long as I have the capability." Labraird smiled and placed the crown on Alaric's head.

"Long and fruitful may be your life and reign, Prince Consort Alaric", he proclaimed.

Then he turned back to the stone and lifted the Ruler's Crown above my head. "Do you swear, ArdRighian Tara, once of Killbrae and now of all Eirlandia, to faithfully perform your duties as ArdRighian of Eirlandia for as long as the people and Forces of Eirlandia deem it?"

"I so swear," I answered. "I never asked for or dreamt of this day, but I will defend and rule my land in justice and equality, with sword and with magic for as long as my people want me and the Spirits give me the power."

With those words, the Crown was placed upon my head, and I suddenly knew the full meaning of my words and my life. I was Eirlandia and She was me, and together we would strive to be the best we could be.

Chapter 18

Maeve looked up from her reading and was astonished, for the day was almost gone. She wouldn't even have time to start out before she would be forced to camp for the night.

"What is it about this book," she wondered "that so catches me up in it that I lose all track of time? It is not in the nature of Fighdrui to be so fixated on one thing."

She had read a great deal of the book, but there was much left and she was running out of time. She still knew nothing of what happened to the Lifenstone and the Crowns. Part of her urged her to simply bring the book to court and let the scholars take over, and some part of her whispered that it was the Old Ones' will that *she* be one to find the Master Lifenstone and bring it's location to her sovereign. Little did she realize her true destiny was something quite different.

The autumn had come and winter storms would be starting soon. There would be no travel to Vikland or anywhere else for several months. Her task had been to find the book and return it. She had to determine if the book mentioned the Master Lifenstone again and where it might be, for she somehow knew that the former Tara's Lifenstone was the key to finding the crowns.

Sighing, she marked the book with a scrap of paper and got up. Slowly stretching, she realized she had not eaten all day, so prepared herself a simple meal from the store of food she had brought. The day was ending and the light fading, so she lit a solitary lamp and laid out her bedding. Luckily there were spare blankets here, so she would not be cold, even though she would refrain from lighting a fire.

Maeve thought back to her time of leaving Kilawey and her last conversation with Aelfund the night before.

Aelfund was the head of her order but also a dear friend who had known her since girlhood. It was unknown how old he actually was, as he didn't appear to age as other men. Still strong, red haired, and in prime fighting condition he could be 30 or 40 or 50 or even older. His outfit of close fitting trews and shirt showed exactly how physically fit he was. His face was only lightly lined, and some whispered he had Sidheran blood that helped him stay young. Maeve didn't know if that was true or not, but in any case he was someone you wanted on your side in any sort of battle, whether it be physical or mental.

"You know I do not wish to send you alone on this mission, Maeve", Aelfund had told her. "But the ArdDrui has told me that only you would have any chance of success in this endeavor. It seems that your genealogy makes you the best candidate for this task. He also mentioned that not only the Crowns should be found, but the Lifestone of the ArdRighian also. Hopefully the Book will hold the answers to both these mysteries.

"Finding the book is your first task," he had continued. "If you feel you need extra time to follow other leads you may come across once you find the Book, you must let me know by Sending. We need the Book before Mid Winter in order to have enough time to search through it and find what we need in order to mount an expedition to retrieve the crowns and, hopefully, the Lifestone also.

"But until then there is no hurry. Use your judgement, I trust you in this. And don't be afraid to call for back up if you need it. Go with my blessings and those of the Old Ones, Maeve. There is more riding on your success than you may understand."

Maeve had nodded her understanding of his instructions, and gone out, wondering what he had meant about her genealogy. She did not know much of her family line, few Fighdrui did. Now she wondered if by chance she had Sidheran blood and that was why the Lifestone seemed so important to her.

Well, it hardly mattered at this moment, she decided. She would skip even farther ahead in the book and try to find the section where Tara began speaking of hiding the crowns and perhaps the Master Lifestone.

From the reading the book, at least she understood more the importance of the Master Lifenstone. While she had heard the term before, she knew there were only a few Lifenstones in existence and that their powers were fairly limited. The ArdRighian had possession of one, but it was not Tara's stone, instead it was the one that had belonged to Labraird, the ArdDrui of first Tara's reign.

Making herself some tea, Maeve sat back down and, again, prayed to the Elder Gods for guidance. She slipped the paper out of the book, then dug her fingers toward the end the volume.

Surely the final days of the Great Revolt would be recorded in the book, and in reading of the days before their deaths, Maeve would find the references she needed. In the morning she would do a Sending, telling Aelfund of her success in finding the book and telling him she was pursuing knowledge of the Lifenstone and would be delayed in returning.

She would also Send that she needed more supplies and that she was taking what was at the waystation so that Aelfund would send someone out with more supplies. The waystations of the Fighdrui were never left bare except for emergencies and were always restocked as soon as possible.

As before, Maeve skimmed pages, skipping whole sections once she figured out the time involved. The years of Tara and Alaric's reign were good years for Eirlandia. The power of the Formorrid had been broken, and the treaty with the Vikes held strong and firm. King Leeife died of old age, and Alaric became King of the Vikes as well as Prince Consort of Eirlandia.

He appointed Skaald Odine as Chancellor/Regent, and the Skaald went back to Vikland to rule in Alaric's stead. The two monarchs visited Vikland often, and Sven was named Heir and Chancelor after Skaald Odine's death. The guard Vilk became head of the Armed Forces of Vikland and also became Sven's best friend and comrade.

The ArdDrui Labraird died of an illness and Cullucan took his place. "Ah," thought Maeve, "I am getting close then." She knew that Cullucan had not been ArdDrui long when the Great Revolt started, that unforeseen rising of some of the heads of the tribes against Tara and Alaric.

It had been found out after the fact that the Formorrid had infiltrated those courts and through their potions and magics had taken over the wills of those Righs who revolted, but the damage to the country had been done, and a new line of Ard-Righs was established, since Tara and Alaric had had no direct heirs. Maeve read with tears in her eyes as the ArdRighian revealed that she and Alaric would have no heir, for the magic she had wielded in order to create the Twin Crowns had stopped her monthly courses, never to be resumed.

Still, the cousin whom the Sidheran had produced had been a good king and his line had ruled Eirlandia well for many generations. The Vikes had had their own new king, of course, in Sven, but relations between the two countries stayed strong for some time before the Formorrid again worked their dark ways and turned the sentiments of the Vikes against the Eirlandians once again, although no war between the nations was ever fought.

Now, once again, the tide was turning, and the present King of Vikland was said to be considering asking for the hand of the ArdRighian in marriage, with the intent of once again combining the rule of Vikland and Eirlandia. Maeve could not help but wonder at the coincidence that these two rulers bore again the names of first two joint rulers.

King Alaric of Vikland and ArdRighian Tara of Eirlandia had met in a neutral nation a few years ago to sign a Declaration of Peace between the two nations. It had appeared to those present, Maeve being one of them, that the two had almost seemed to know each other, even though they had never met.

The mutual attraction was obvious to all present, and it came as no surprise this last Spring when King Alaric had formally requested the hand of Tara in marriage and assured her of his intent to be only her consort in Eirlandia as she would be his in Vikland.

The only caveat to this proposal was the stipulation that the Ruling Crowns be found and the couple re-coronated on their wedding day as joint rulers of Eirlandia and Vikland. The crowns bore Lifestones, she knew, but the Master Stone had been separate, and held the key, she was sure, to the success of the finding of the Crowns.

Maeve sipped her tea and turned the pages, scanning quickly. She didn't need anything before the time just before the Last Battle, when the Royal Consort and ArdRighian had lost their lives. She knew they had hidden the crowns just before then and, she assumed, the Master Lifenstone also. If they had had those objects, perhaps the battle would not have been lost. Had the battle had gone differently, then the whole history of the nation could have changed. However, Maeve knew the Ruling Crowns and the Master Lifenstone had been taken out of play, as the future had not been assured. Tara and Alaric wanted to make sure the objects were safe from discovery by by the enemy. For example, had the objects fallen into the hands of the Formorrid, Maeve was sure that her country would not still exist.

Maeve skipped even further ahead. She was close to end of the book now, but not too close. She knew she needed to be a few weeks or more before the battle. She wasn't sure when ArdRighian Tara last wrote in the book or even if the last entries were by someone else, and she resisted the temptation to go to the very end and find out. She scanned quickly, and read snatches regarding the start of the rebellion and the loss of lives on both sides.

"It seems our time here is almost done", Maeve read. "The council has fled, many turning from me and Alaric, victims of the lies that have been spread about us. Soon we will have to fight our own people, and my heart grows heavy at the thought. I will not use the Lifenstone against my own. It will be sent away, where it can do no harm and where, perhaps, it will be found again by another ruler and used to again right wrongs in another time."

"At last," Maeve breathed. "Tell me, Tara, where did you send the precious stone?"

Chapter 19

A NEW DAY HAD DAWNED. Maeve had resisted the temptation to continue reading the night before. Her eyes were tired and she didn't want to miss anything important. Sighing, she had prepared for bed, taking a dose of herbal tea to help her sleep.

Awakening refreshed, she prepared a light breakfast of oats and dried berries, along with more tea, this time a brew to keep her focus sharp. After breakfast she cleaned up and took the book outside to the small porch, where the fall sunshine was bright and she did not have to use up the lamps for her reading. Settling herself comfortable in the chair, she opened the book and again began to read…

Very soon, I fear, I shall no longer write in this journal. I have told about our struggles; how some of our Righs were taken in by lies and are even now marching toward us. Our loyal troops and the Drui are doing their best to delay them without large loss of life. I detest the thought of civil war, and I will not kill those who come unless I have no choice.

For this reason, I am hiding away the Master Lifenstone. I do not want to be tempted to use its power against my own people. Tonight I will make a journey, such as never before been taken.

I will go with my mother's sister to the Forbidden Realm, the heart of the Sidheran, where only the Master Mages are usually allowed. I go to bring to the Sidheran the greatest treasure in this land, and to ask their help in concealing the second greatest treasures, our crowns.

I do not wish either the Master Lifenstone or the Ruling Crowns to be worn by those who come after us, until such time as Alaric and I again walk this earth and can again take up these instruments of magical power to continue this work which we have begun.

That Alaric and I will live again has already been foretold. I know we live in a cycle of lives, and I know our cycles are not yet over. We have ruled and lived a goodly time in this cycle, but there are still things to be done and even if this war had not come, we could not have lived long enough to do it all. Nor could all that we wish for both Eirlandia and Vikland have been possibly accomplished in one short lifetime. No, the Great Ones understand that some things need more than one life to accomplish. I know that Alaric and I will live again on some distant day, but I hope that we will again come together so that the work we have begun here will not take too long to be finished.

I have determined where I will place my Lifestone. How I will do this deed is what I do not know. Mayveer says none but a full Sidheran has ever walked in the Forbidden Realm, and even the Master Mages do so at great peril and only in great need, for the ways of the Forbidden Realm are not our ways.

But this will be the safest place in all the realms for the Master Lifestone, so great is its magic and power. I am frightened, for while I will visit the Sidheran realm in my body, I will not visit the Forbidden Realm so. Only in the spirit may I walk the paths of that place, and how I will place a physical object somewhere while incorporeal, I have no idea. I can only assume the Mages know the way of this, since they have agreed to help me.

The writing stopped there, and Maeve swore the spots on the page were the remains of tears. Turning the page, she read on.

I am dressed in the simplest of gowns. I wear no jewelry except the Master Lifestone upon my breast. It lies quiet now, but I still can feel its hidden power. Looking up from this journal, I see Alaric at the window. His face is drawn and pale. He does not wish me to undertake this journey. He does not understand why I must do this.

We spoke long into the night last night, and I know he still isn't satisfied with my answers and reasons, but I have no more to tell him. This is something I simply know and cannot fully explain. I do not worry, really, about being lost in the Forbidden Realm, as seers greater than I have already foretold the manner of our deaths. We will die together, back to back, and we will be the agents of our own deaths, for we will call upon powers we would normally transmit through Lifestone or Crown straight through ourselves, for only in that way will we be able to save the land from total destruction.

The exact way of it is yet unknown, but I know how I die, and it will not be tonight in the Realm of the Sidheran, but will, instead, be in the bright light of day and on the Hill of Kincordia.

Again the page ended abruptly, and Maeve turned to the next entry.

I have done what must be done and, since I still live, will tell now how this deed was accomplished. I do not worry about others reading this after me and somehow finding the Lifestone, for the Realm of the Sidheran is secret in itself and the Forbidden Realm secret even from most of Sidheran.

They will be ones to decide when to reveal the dwelling place of the Master Lifestone, and to whom. The Lifestone is no longer my concern, but I write this account so that, when the time comes and this book is found, the steps it describes can be given to the Seeker so that the Sidheran will know the Seeker is the true Heir and will reveal to her the hiding place of the Master Lifestone, although she will still have to brave the terrors of the Forbidden Realm.

When the door was opened, I saw Alaric, Daman, Mayveer and Cullucan standing in the hallway. Like myself, Mayveer was dressed very simply. For the first time I realized that she, too, owned a Lifenstone, for it hung in plain sight on her gown, blazing brightly. Her hair was drawn up and away from her face for first time also, and I saw the point to her ears that marked her Sidheran more than another other physical feature.

Alaric, Daman and Cullucan would, I knew, accompany me only as far as the chamber in the Sidheran realm where my body would lie while my spirit journeyed with the Stone to the Forbidden Realm.

Mayveer, on the other hand, would travel with me, for she was only one of a few who knew the ways of that place and the only one who would agree to lead me. I had been told the other Sidheran mages were reluctant to allow this, but she was a Principea, a powerful Mage and my aunt, all of which carried much weight in the High Council. So it had been decided that I be allowed this, since the hiding away of the Master Lifenstone was something all wished accomplished, and, in the end, all agreed that the Forbidden Realm was the best place to do it.

Mayveer actually smiled, which put me somewhat at ease. "Do not be frightened, my sister's daughter," she said in Eirl. "The way is not so terrible and I will be there to guide you. No harm will come to you, although you will feel weak for a while afterwards both because of the journey and also because you will no longer have the strength of the Lifenstone with you to call upon at need."

"Tara, my Love" said Alaric then," take my arm and let us go. My soul is chilled with the thoughts of what you do tonight, but I know all will be well and I understand the reasons for it. I and Daman and Cullucan will guard you with physical and magical means, although I certainly expect no attack, especially not in Sidhera."

I took my love's hand, then, and smiled at him. No matter what happened, I knew Alaric would be faithful and would protect me. I had no fear of dying that night, I knew I would survive; I only hoped I would survive whole in mind, body and spirit for no one had ever attempted what I was now set to do.

We traveled first through normal, well lit corridors. I knew the Nemed well, and thought I knew all of its secrets by now. But I was shown wrong. We came to a wall that I thought at first was a wrong turning, a dead end, but Mayveer held up her stone and spoke some sort of phrase that opened the wall. What I mean by that is that the wall just seemed to disappear completely. There was no sound, no movement of the stone, it was simply there one moment, and replaced by a corridor leading onward into darkness in another.

"And that which is hidden is revealed for the Prophesied One", she told me in High Eirl as we passed through. "Remember that phrase, commit it to memory. You must pass this saying down through the ages so your successor will it." And I have, and I write the translation here. My successor will know

High Eirl, and so know the first of the passwords is passed.

As we walked, I realized that Mayveer's stone was sending out enough light to easily see by, although it was a strange blue-tinged light. The walls here were only rough stone and dirt, more of a tunnel than any finished corridor. Cool breezes touched my cheek on occasion, and I almost felt as if soft hands touched me from time to time.

Alaric shivered and held me closer. A soft, insistent murmuring occurred in my head, and I felt they were telling me something, but I didn't understand what. I somehow knew, however, that these were the voices of my ancestor Sidherans, come to guide and protect me on my journey.

I cannot say why I think that, but in light of the fact that I was spared some of the terrible visions I had heard could happen in the Forbidden Realm, I can only assume I was somehow protected.

A glance at Alaric's white face told me that he, however, was not protected, and was probably experiencing some unpleasant sensations.

"It is alright, my Love" I murmured in Vike. "They are but shades of beings long gone and cannot hurt you. They have come to protect me and surely see you as no threat. Be at ease, these are not like your Vikland demons, who haunt the hidden passes in winter, ready to ensnare the unwary. Be at ease, for you walk with the one whom these spirits seek to protect."

I felt his hand unclench a little then, and knew he had taken my words to heart. Behind me I heard the other two men murmuring in low tones, but I could make out none of the words. I don't think they were conversing but were, instead, each saying prayers and incantations of protection against whatever the Sidheran ancestors were doing to them.

"Be at ease, oh my worthy predecessors", I said in Eirl softly. "These men travel with me for my protection. Do them no harm." At my words, it seemed the forces withdrew, for the atmosphere immediately became less charged and fearful.

Mayveer looked back and smiled approvingly. "The Ancestors are pleased." She said. "You thought of the others besides yourself. You have passed the test and have been shown worthy to enter the Forbidden Realm. We are almost at the outer chamber. Come, all of you, warmth and light and refreshment await us."

With that we all hurried forward that much faster and, turning a corner, found ourselves in a somewhat large cavern. It was obviously natural, but steam issued from several small vents and couches and tables with food and drink were evident, as were glowing lights, the like of which I seen only in the Formorrid Dun.

As if she could read my mind, Mayveer addressed the subject of the lights. "These may look familiar to you, Alaric and Tara. The Formorrid stole this secret of the lights from us in the Last Great War. It is a small enough thing, and we do not begrudge them.

In fact much of what we have and had developed we would have shared freely with the Formorrid, but they chose to disbelieve us and tried to take what they wanted by force. They came away with precious little, but the knowledge of the lamps was one of their small victories."

Her light extinquished itself, and she led us to a smaller chamber that held two couches. Between the beds was a sitting chair and small tables were on either side. Mayveer chose the bed on her right and sat down, taking off her Lifenstone and placing it on the table next to the bed. She indicated the other bed to me with a nod of her head.

"Lay yourself down, Tara, and remove the Lifenstone from the chain around your neck, but hold it firmly in your hands. Place the stone so it rests on your chest and you hands cover it." As I did as she commanded, she continued.

"Alaric, you and Daman go into the outer chamber for just a bit. ArdDrui Cullucan and I must prepare Tara and then she and I must begin our journey. When Cullucan is satisfied we are on our way, he will come tell you so you may come and watch over us."

Alaric came to me and bent down, kissing me fiercely. "Do not get yourself killed, Tara", he said in Vike, "or I swear I will come looking for you on the other side and damned be those that try to stop me."

"I will not die here, Alaric" I assured him. "We yet have our final destinies to fulfill."

"I am not sure I believe your visions" he told me. "But if you promise me you will live, I will take that vow and hold you to it, Wooeden as my witness."

"I promise," I answered. "Now go, for the sooner this is done the sooner we can return home and to our marriage bed." And I grinned wickedly and winked.

Alaraic laughed softly. "Ever my little Eaglet, aren't you?" he murmured as he strode through the entry way.

Mayveer laughed softly. "Alright, sister's daughter, now relax and close your eyes. Try to form the picture of the Lifenstone in your mind and hold it there. You will feel, probably, many strange sensations, but do not open your eyes, or speak, or even move until I tell you. What Cucullan and I do here has never been done, and I can only hope that the Ancestor Spirits will guide and help us, for we will surely fail without them."

I closed my eyes and imagined the Lifenstone as I had seen it that morning on the hilltop against the Formorrid, blazing with light.

I cannot describe adequately what, exactly, I felt. The sensation was almost one of falling, but I knew with a piece of my mind that I was still in the bed in the chamber deep underground and there was no where to fall. Sensation seemed to desert me at one point, except for my hands, which I could still feel were tightly clutched around the Lifenstone.

Murmurs again sounded, but they seemed a chorus of voices, almost of the sea in a cave, whispering its age old secrets to rocks. Then the sound almost of a waterfall, a roaring, deep sound that almost enveloped me, and then all was deathly still and quiet.

"Open your eyes, Tara, and gaze upon the Forbidden Realm." I heard Mayveer say. "We have done it, now we must reach the central well and return back here in the allotted time, or we shall perish here and our bodies be but empty shells for as many days at it takes to starve."

Those words shocked my eyes open. The first thing I saw was Mayveer, only not Mayveer. She was as beautiful as ever, only moreso, and she had a luminous cloud around her and she seemed almost translucent.

"Whaa?" I started to say.

"You see my spirit, Niece" she said in answer to my unfinished word. "You are the same, although you will seem the same to yourself, for we can never see our own spirit in the same manner as others do. You still hold the Lifenstone, you must let it guide you now to its resting place. This was where it was created, and it will know how to get to the Central Well the best.

Hold it up, its light will guide us now."

I took the Lifenstone and held it as she commanded. The light made a beam that crossed the space above us and shown on a distant place that looked something like a tower.

"Good," declared Mayveer. "Now, command the Lifenstone to keep the tower lit, but to light our way through the labyrinth. Do it silently, the Lifenstone will hear you, and remember to speak in Eirl."

I did has she commanded and a second beam shown out from the stone, lighting the path before us. "The beam will show us where to go, if we come to a crossroads, it will light the turning we must take," I told Mayveer, sure of my knowledge, even though I knew not where the knowledge came from.

"Then let us start off," she responded. "We will not need to eat or drink or rest here, and you will find we will travel more swiftly than in our bodies. We can also cross places that would not be possible in physical form. But we still have a ways to travel and hazards to overcome between here and there.

All travel in the Forbidden Realm is a test of our inner selves, and the spirits of this place have no mercy on those whose inner strength is not great enough for the challenge." Those ominous words ringing in my ears, we took off at a lively pace, letting the beam guide us.

Even as I write these words, the specifics of this journey begin to fade. I know that we turned left at the first crossing and came to a mighty river. Here we had to simply 'will' ourselves across, but I swear I could feel the rushing spray on my face, and I felt cold and wet for some time afterwards.

The path did not run in a straight line, but was fairly straight forward for some ways. The second turning was marked by what appeared to be an ancient oak. Here we followed a line of trees, oak, ash, thorn, elder, birch and others, all the sacred trees, to a grove.

The grove was empty and we saw our path almost straight across from where we entered. But getting there was not as easy at it seemed. Shades of the dead came to us, asking questions, trying to impede us, setting traps that we had to avoid without losing too much time.

Without Mayveer, I do not know if I could have surmounted this test, for I saw my brother and father, as well as those who had died in that terrible battle with the Formorrid so many years ago.

But we reached the other side and headed back into a wooded area, which lead up to higher ground. We could not see what lay ahead, but Mayveer kept urging me to hurry, saying she felt we were almost there and that our time was running out.

Topping a rise, we suddenly saw the tower and the large well in front of it. There appeared to be no more impediments and we ran down the hill into the glen. The stone was blazing now, literally pulling me forward. At the edge of the well was a case of almanite and silver, the top already open. A deep cushion of felt was inside and I gently laid the Lifenstone within. The light dimned to almost nothing, but then I noticed that the tower appeared to gleam with its own light, so we were not left in darkness. I closed the case and looked at Mayveer, unsure what to do next.

"Consign the case and Lifenstone to the Well of Life. It will not be harmed. As you drop it, tell the well who it must next allow to retrieve the Lifenstone, lest it remain here forever. Do this silently, for even I must not know what limits and conditions you put upon this, so that I am not tempted, in some future life, to come back and try to retrieve it myself."

And so I told the Well what it must seek. I cannot write this down, but I swear that The One Who Is To Come will know the words and will past the test of the Forbidden Realm and retrieve the Lifenstone at the correct time and place.

Once the case and stone was out of sight, I turned to Mayveer. "We no longer have a guide, how do we get out in time?"

She smiled knowingly. "The way out is much easier than the journey within," she said. "Come, let us climb the opposite hill and you will see what I mean."

So we journeyed up the hill and, to my amazement, there, just a short distance away, was the door that led into the chamber where Mayveer and I, in our physical forms, rested.

We walked to the door, slid through and looked upon our sleeping forms. Alaric was seated beside me and Cullucan beside Mayveer, both keeping vigil.

"Watch what I do" said Mayveer. "I have taken this journey a few times before. Coming back is not hard, but can be disorienting. Do not worry if you feel very tired when your physical body awakes. Drink and eat, even though you will not want to. You will feel better quickly."

Then she walked to her body and climbed into the bed, laying herself down and disappearing back into her physical self. Her body gave a sudden deep breath and her eyes opened.

"Now, Tara," she commanded. Then her eyes closed again.

I walked to my body, past Alaric who was staring in amazement at Mayveer, and also slipped inside. I cannot put into words the feeling that came over me. I felt my heart beat and my lungs breathe in the air. I smelled Alaric and the mulled wine he held to my lips, and tasted what seemed to be the drink of the gods to my newly awakened sense of taste. I opened my eyes then and smiled.

"I am to have food," I whispered to him. "I think some cheese and bread would be good."

Alaric's eyes widened, but then he smiled and lifted me up a little while he piled pillows behind me. "Here is fresh cheese and bread and some mulled wine. Cullucan said you would ask for these, and I didn't believe him. I wasn't even sure you were still alive, so still were you, and you seemed not to breathe and I felt no heart beat."

"My spirit was journeying, so the body was empty for a bit" I told him. "Your presence here kept me safe from those Otherworld Beings who would have used this chance to take over my body. I have returned, and I will not take this journey again in This Life."

"The Master Lifestone is gone from your hands", Cullucan remarked. "I take it your journey was successful."

"Indeed," I answered. "The Lifestone is safe in the Well of Life until we have need of it again in Another Time. Now we have but to make arrangements for the Crowns once we are gone. I know, good friend, that you will see to them."

"I will indeed," he answered. "And you must remember to put down clues as to their whereabouts before you and Alaric partake in the Final Battle. I will be there and will see the crowns safe to their place when the time comes, but it is you who must provide the clues to the Future Heir."

"As well I know", I answered. "I will think on this and devise some clues that will lead to the crowns while at the same time assuring that only the One who is so fated will be able to retrieve them."

And so I ate and rested, as did Mayveer. Soon we felt stronger and we left the Realm of the Sidheran to return to Eirlandia. At least, Alaric, Cullucan and I did.

Mayveer stayed behind, saying that she was now ruler in Sidhera, and she would organize her people's part in the last battle and see to their safety and survival no matter what the outcome 'above world', as she put it.

So now the tale of the Lifestone is done. When next I write, I shall speak of the Crowns and their fate.

Maeve looked up from the book, tears in her eyes. She had had no idea of the sacrifice Tara had made in concealing the Lifestone. The story of the ArdRighian's journey left her feeling amost as if she had traveled to the Forbidden Realm. She was almost afraid to read about the Last Battle and the Ultimate Sacrifice which ended with Tara and Alaric giving up their lives in order to keep the Crowns safe. She knew the history, certainly, but she wasn't sure she could stand reading it in the ArdRighian's own hand.

And then she thought about it. "How can the ArdRighian write what happened to the Crowns when she died protecting them?" she wondered to herself. "Is the last part of this journal the ArdRighian's writings or someone else? Is it a mixture of both, perhaps? If the ArdRighian and Consort died wearing the crowns, how would Tara know what happened to them? Are our stories of that time even accurate? Should I simply bring this back to Kilawey and let my ArdRighian Tara sort it out?" The questions ran through her head over and over, but she could come to no answer.

"I've read too much to simply stop now" she finally decided. "The story is almost done. When I know the truth I can return to ArdRighian Tara and tell her what I know, thereby sparing her the pain of reading this for herself."

The decision made, Maeve took a moment to make tea and to eat. Then, settling herself as comfortably as possible, she opened the book for what she assumed would be last time and began to read.

"I write these words with sorrow.," Maeve read. "My beloved Eirlandia is in dire trouble, and I fear she will not be the same land for a long time. A chapter of her history is ending, and I am but a pawn of Fate in this story.

Tonight I must use all the power I possess to create a lie. And no one must know of it, except my faithful Cullucan.

Not even Alaric must suspect my duplicity, and that wounds me to my core. For the future of this land, however, the veil must be drawn over my doings so that no one can give away the secret.

In the Dark Hour I will take the Sacred Crowns and hide them, with Cullucan's help, in a place that only my future Self will be able to return to. I pray I am right in believing that I will again walk the sweet lands of Eirlandia and that Alaric will once again walk at my side. For if I am wrong, I will have possibly condemned my land to eternal darkness and strife.

And when I have done this deed, I must make a mock set of crowns for us to wear in battle, and they must seem to all eyes and senses to be the real things. It is these that people will see removed from our heads by Culcullan and secreted away in yet another secret place. I would write this not at all except Culcullan has assured me he will put this book in a place that only a special person, called by Fate, would be able to find and open.

From the twinkle in his eye when he said this, I gather it will be a spot that is hidden in plain site, for Culcullan loves to play with people's minds.

You who read these words, know that the Hidden Vale is known only to the Ard-Righs and ArdRighians of Eirlandia from time out of mind. No power on earth or in the underworld can be used to locate this vale unless the Anointed Seeker is present. To the future Seeker I say these words, and only you will understand them.

"Seek the place where the light does shine but once a year. Within the darkness hides the Guide who is both terrible and powerful. To disturb the Guide is to court disaster, so tread with light steps and find the passage to the Chamber of the Ancestors. Within yourself shall you find written the Path of Salvation and at the end of that Path is the goal you seek."

Know, too, that only with the help of the MasterLifenstone will you be able to retrieve the True Crowns. Also, the False Crowns will hold within themselves other clues to the whereabouts of the True Crowns. Seek and find those first, then the Master Lifenstone, then the True Crowns. Only in this order will you succeed. The blessings of the Greater Beings upon you and upon this land and that of Vikland. I pray with all my being that, someday, Eirlandia and Vikland will again unite, this time permanently and that, together, they shall usher in a new Golden Age such as the world has never known.

I will write no more in this book. I will be too exhausted after the Workings to do more than sleep;

and I know I will not survive this battle. I know that the Drui will see that the story of the Battle is recorded, and Cucullan will see to the hiding of the False Crowns and the construction of the riddle that will reveal them.

All that can be done to ensure the future of Eirlandia has or will be done before I seek the solace of the Other World and await a new life here in Eirlandia.

I wonder how this land and people will have changed by the time I see them again? Oh, well, I shall have much to ponder in my Next Life, won't I?

Farewell, all my Beloveds. I will see you again someday.

Chapter 20

Maeve closed the book, slowly, tears in her eyes. She felt both satisfied that she had finished the book, and somewhat angry that she knew little more now than when she had started reading days ago.

Yes, she would be able to save the scholars time by showing them the passages that were most helpful in figuring out how to find the missing Master Lifenstone and Crowns; but she would still have nothing but this book to give to her Tara.

In the end, she felt as if she had simply wasted time in this task. Or, at least part of her thought that. Another part still marveled at the story of the First Tara, of her courage and her skill and power.

Maeve hoped that she would be able to have the leisure to read the entire journal again some day, and not skip over the years that spoke of the founding of the Eirelandia-Vikland coallision. Still, she had here and now to deal with and the future would just have to take care of itself.

She checked the time, and decided she would simply start for home in the morning instead of doing a Sending. Oh, she would Send, but only to say she was halfway home and to have someone meet her with a fresh horse so she could return all the quicker.

It was obvious from the writing that the next steps of the journey would be Tara's to make, and Maeve did not envy her mistress the task. The scholars would have to figure out where the False Crowns were hidden, and retrieve them. Perhaps the ArdDrui would be helpful in that, for surely his predescessors would have passed down the knowledge of the loction of the False Crown.

After the False Crowns were retrieved and their secrets revealed, Tara would have to figure out how to journey to the Forbidden Realm to retrieve the Master Lifenstone. Finally, Tara would have to figure out the final clues regarding the True Crowns, journey to their hiding places and return safely to Kilawey in time to accomplish her plan to unite Eirlandia and Vikland once again before the next End of Harvest. A Full Cycle seemed both a long time and a very short time to get all this done.

Maeve packed her things to be ready to leave at first light, and lay down on the bedding. Closing her eyes, she breathed a prayer to the Ancestors to watch over her and over ArdRighian Tara until all could be accomplished.

Then she slipped into the Realm of Sleep and knew no more until the birds again awoke her to a new day.

The morning was bright and clear, which made Maeve smile. The weather was holding, it seemed, and she could only hope it would continue to do so until she again reached Kilawey.

Going outside, she climbed a small hill nearby and sat in the light of the rising sun. Putting herself into the light trance that accompanied a Sending, she sought out Aelfund.

"Greetings, Maeve" she heard Aelfund say in her mind. "It has been enough time that I was beginning to worry. Were you successful?"

"Moreso than we could have imagined," she answered in turn. "I have skimmed the Book of Tara and found out we need the Master Lifenstone and that there are two sets of crowns and we need them all if the plan is to be successful."

"Another Lifenstone? Why?" asked Aelfund

"The one ArdRighian Tara has is not the Master Lifenstone," she answered. "The Master Stone was sealed away in a place in Sidhera called the Forbidden Realm. ArdRighian Tara has to spirit journey back there to retrieve it. It is complicated, and I will tell you more when I come.

"Please send a runner and a fresh horse down the path to the Third Way Station and I will meet him there. He will also need to bring supplies to restock the Fourth station for what I used."

The Sending finished, Maeve stumbled back down the hill and rested for a little bit. Sending was hard when you didn't do it often, and Maeve had never been far enough away from Kilawey before to need to use that mental discipline.

She had always been able to rely on her birds and other messengers, but the trip here had necessitated not bringing any one or anything else along in case of traps or other things. She had even had to make the last five miles or so by foot instead of on horseback.

Much had been rumored about the old Library in the Nemed at Kilawey, and just about all of it wrong. Maeve would be telling her story many times to many different people when she returned so that records could be updated and teams of scholars sent to the library to shift through the debris to find what treasures might still lay hidden under the rubble.

About an hour later, Maeve felt strong enough to shoulder her tote and the bag containing the Book and start off toward the next Way Station, where, hopefully, a horse would be waiting to speed her return to Kilawey.

Although Aelfund had not responded to her request, Maeve knew that he would have commanded a horse and rider be sent immediately. Only if he had been unable to comply would he have Sent back to her.

She walked through a land on the edge of winter. The wind was cool, but the sun was shining. The few fields she skirted were stripped of their harvest. The New Year had just occurred, and all would be preparing for the long nights and short days of the Dark Time.

Maeve kept alert, but felt no inkling of problems anywhere in her area. The road was wide and well maintained. The Kingdom was not as wealthy or powerful as in the old Tara's day, but it was still peaceable enough in the interior, where raiders never penetrated.

Cresting a hill in mid afternoon, Maeve spotted the next Waystation. This was much larger than the one she had spent the last night in. This was a permanent Fighdrui station, with a large barn for the messenger horses and other animals that were used by the Fighdrui in their roles as Royal Spies, Messengers and even, sometimes, Stealth Fighters.

She could see smoke rising from the chimney and it looked like several horses where loose in the coral adjoining the barn, not having been put into their stalls for night yet. Anticipating a good meal and warm mead, Maeve increased her pace, planning to reach the station before the late autumn sun set.

About two thirds of the way there, Maeve heard the sound of a horse being ridden fast coming from her left. There was another road joining hers just a ways ahead, and it was obvious whoever was on the horse was on that road.

Maeve hurried to the crossing, then stepped out of road to the side, standing silent and almost invisible in the shadows of the trees around her. She felt no inkling of concern, but it was best to be safe, and if the rider was coming as fast as it seemed, they might not see her in time.

In a few moments a rider did indeed appear, coming at a swift pace on what was obviously a Royal Steed. The rider kept looking backwards, as if expecting to see something, though no followers were in sight.

Nearing the crossing, the rider pulled up on the reigns, slowing slightly. Maeve felt it safe to reveal herself, and stepped back into the roadway, although she stood at very edge and away from where the horse would turn.

The effect was startling and unexpected. The messenger's eyes widened and the horse almost stopped in mid step, rearing up in panic.

A beam from the messenger's weapon went by Maeve just a fingerwidth away from striking her. Maeve stood her ground and threw back her cloak so the stranger could see the Fighdrui emblem sewn on her tunic.

She knew she wasn't well known to the outlying Fighdrui, and assumed the rider had been startled enough to assume her a problem. The beam, even if it had struck, would not have killed her, only rendered her unconscious for a time.

Controlling the horse, the messenger stopped and stared hard at her a moment. "Who are you?" he demanded harshly. "And what are you doing on that road? No one travels that path unless they have come from the Disputed Lands. You wear the Crest of the Figdrui, but I have heard of no one of our clan being in the Disputed Lands for some time."

Maeve held her weapon hand up in peace, and spread her cloak so he could see she was weaponless. "I am Maeve, Fighdrui to ArdRighian Tara herself. I have been on a confidential royal mission to the

Great Library on the edge of the Disputed Lands and am now returning to Kilawey. I look to spent the night at the Waystation. Do you travel there also?"

The messenger cocked his head, as if listening, then looked up to where a spy eagle sat perched in a tree above Maeve, hidden almost completely by the foliage.

Maeve followed his gaze and chided herself for not sensing the bird's nearness. The bird swooped down and onto to the waiting arm of the messenger.

"This is Lugh" he said, indicating the bird. "He tells me you speak truthfully. He also says you hold a secret in your pouch, and I am anxious to hear your tale regarding it."

Suddenly he smiled, and his whole face changed. "I am called Talisean," he said. "I bring important news to the Council and ArdRighian regarding the movements of the Displaced. Ride with me, for I too journey to the First Station for the night."

Maeve smiled back and easily mounted the horse. Talisean moved forward at a good but not speeding pace. "My news is time sensitive," he told her, "and I have been followed part of the way here. I seem to have lost them, however. I take it you are riding to Kilawey also? We can journey together come the morrow, if you wish." He smiled, turning back toward her. "I am sorry about my reaction. Things are getting tense in the outlying areas, and you startled me."

Maeve smiled back, "I understand. It was partially my fault, I should have given a sign I was there before I moved as I did." She shrugged. "I don't have a lot of field experience and I am a little rusty."

Talisean nodded and urged the horse to a slightly faster pace. "I wish to get to the station as soon as possible. They have been putting up barriers come nightfall and we need to reach the limits of the station before those are activated or we might not get in."

Maeve was quiet, there seemed no need to reply, though she wondered what had happened to put the Fighdrui on such a high alert status. Was the situation more grave than she had been led to believe? Or had things moved rapidly in her absence? She wished she could just transport herself back to Kilawey that instant. But even the most powerful Drui could not bring other than themselves such a distance; and it was the Book that was the most precious.

They traveled the rest of the way in silence. The Station was well provisioned and even had a Caretaker who provided food, baths and decent beds for the two of them.

Maeve had said nothing to Talisean about the Book or her adventures, and he had not pushed. She hadn't asked about his news either, assuming that both of them needed to report to their superiors first before making any knowledge known to others, even other Fighdrui.

Maeve wasn't even sure if Talisean was a Fighdrui or something else. She assumed he was Drui of some sort since he had a Spy Bird, but one could never be sure.

The two talked about the weather and Talisean was able to tell her that things were tense but had not erupted into fighting, at least not yet. Talisean stole some glances at her pouch, but said nothing further. Maeve noted that Lugh was not with them, and assumed the bird had been sent ahead to tell of their coming.

The following night was spent in the open, but the weather had actually warmed unexpectedly, and Maeve was fairly comfortable. Tomorrow would see her in Kilawey, and she was fervently wishing she could somehow wish herself into the Royal Dun right that moment. "The sooner I can get this information to ArdRighian Tara and the Council, the more chance I have of helping find the Crowns", she thought to herself as she settled in for the night.

She dreamt of the original Tara that night. It seemed the ArdRighian was trying to tell her something, but no words came out.

The ArdRighian kept pointing to a towering mountain that Maeve was not sure she had ever seen before. "Beneath the roots", Tara kept mouthing. "The Way lies beneath the roots".

Then the dream faded and Maeve slept dreamless the remainder of the night. In the morning the dream was forgotten, and Maeve was up early, saddling the horse she had received at the Station.

"I must travel as quickly as possible" she told a sleepy Talisean. "I will see you at the Nemed. Come to the Royal Enclosure when you are done with your report and ask for me. We will have a nice drink and tell each other our stories.

"But the ArdRighian needs this information, as does the ArdDrui and the council, as quickly as possible. We are under a time constraint it seems, and there is more work to be done before all can be revealed and the deeds accomplished."

So saying, she finished securing the bags and mounted. "May the roads rise up to meet you, the wind be at your back, and the sun shine warm on your face" she intoned.

"May the Great Ones hold you in the palms of their hands," Talisean replied. It was the standard farewell of all Fighdrui, which told Maeve one of the things she had wondered, Talisean was indeed of the Fighdrui.

"Until Kilawey, then" she said.

"Until Kilawey", he answered.

Maeve turned her mount's head the headed down the path to the road, where she let the steed loose and almost flew down the road. The steed was one of the Runner Breed, who could go at a fast pace for hours without losing breath or stride. They were used mostly by messengers, but Maeve had claimed one for this last leg, knowing that speed was going to be essential.

Chapter 21

Maeve reached the Royal Nemed in almost record time, she estimated. Moving swiftly, she sent a servant to inform the Head Fighdrui, The ArdDrui and The ArdRighian of her return.

"Tell them I will meet them after I have washed from my travels and had a small meal," she told the servant. She could tell from the boy's expression that he was startled that she would so order the ArdRighian and her advisors, but he nodded and went to do her bidding.

Maeve smiled grimly. She had more power than almost anyone in the Nemed knew about, other than those three. They would understand the reason for her delay.

She strode into her rooms, calling for a bath and stripping her clothing as she went. The satchel with the book had already been sent to the ArdRighian as soon as she entered the gates. With luck Tara and her advisors would be pouring over it; another reason she knew she had time for a few personal matters.

After a good cleaning, a small but decent meal, and the donning of fresh clothing, Maeve felt refreshed and ready to face the next part of her task. Placing the symbol of her rank around her neck, she strode through the Nemed, nodding briefly to those she passed whose rank was equal to or greater to her own.

Within a few moments she was entering the ArdRighian's private quarters, the guards already swinging the doors shut behind her. Maeve stepped into the parlor and stopped dead.

There, sitting with Tara, and in deep conference with Master Aelfund and ArdDrui Ealaroth, was none other than Talisean.

Hearing the door, the four of them looked up. Tara smiled broadly. "Ah, my wonderful Maeve, welcome home. Your mission was a great success I see. And I hear you have much more to tell us. Come, sit here next to me. I know you have just eaten, but would you like some mead?"

"A drink is in order, I believe", Maeve answered, still in shock from seeing Talisean. Maeve sat and accepted a goblet from Aelfund. She sipped, not taking her eyes of the man she had assumed to be a simple messenger, but who was clearly more by look of things.

"My apologies for keeping my complete identity secret, Maeve," Talisean said after the silence began to grow awkward. Slowly he drew back his hair from his face, and she saw the pointed ears that marked a Sidheran, although they were somewhat rounded.

"I was on mission, and had my own secrets to keep. My true nature is not known to many here, and must be kept that way.

"I am ArdRighian Tara's half brother, born of a Sidheran mother from a dalliance the old King had before he ever married. I was raised by the Sidheran and taught all a prince needs to know.

"When Tara came to the throne I came here in secret, with letters and proof of my identity and offered her my services as spy, messenger and other things as needed. I have mostly been gone keeping peace in the various clans, allowing Tara the time to consolidate her power as well as finding and learning to wield the power of the Ruling Crowns when needed."

"My good Talisean is very talented in many things, and will be of great help in the next step of our plan," added Tara. "Since he lived in Sidhera for many years, he can help me get to the Forbidden Land and find the Master Lifenstone. I have you to thank, Maeve, for finding out about that, and how important it is."

"Retrieving the Master Lifenstone will be Tara and Talisean's task" chimed in Aelfund. "But your role in this is not through. As a Fighdrui, you must be the one to find the Ruling Crowns and return them to Tara. She will not be able to be gone long enough to do the rest of the hunting herself. Once she has the Lifenstone, you will seek out the Ruling Crowns, using the power of the Lifenstone to help you."

"But the Book said we must find both crowns, the false and the true," Maeve protested. "And the false crowns must be found first, then the Lifenstone and then the true crowns, in that order. I remember reading that clearly."

Aelfund smiled benignly. "Do not trouble yourself over that," he told her. "The false crowns were retrieved by the Drui once it was confirmed that the girl child born to the last king was indeed the reincarnation of the original ArdRighian Tara. That is why our ArdRighian was given her name, a name no girl child in all of Eirlandia has been given since the death of the Great ArdRighian Tara.

"The false crowns are being examined as we speak by the best minds in the kingdom and soon they will yield their secrets about the whereabouts of the Ruling Crowns. Once Tara has the Master Lifenstone and returns it here, your journey will begin."

"This will be a long and ardous journey and one that must be accomplished in as short a time as possible," continued Aelfund. "While you are gone searching, we will be bringing King Alaric here in secret. As soon as the crowns are found and returned, the two shall marry and be crowned. We must accomplish this as quickly as possible, before the rebellious Righs completely unite and possibly even find a way to bring the Formorrid in to help them."

"The Formorrid?" Maeve questioned. "I thought they were long gone."

"Unfortunately, no" answered the ArdDrui Elaroth. "Although they were severely weakened in the original Tara's time, the intervening centuries have allowed them to regain much of their strength.

Their special abilities are not as formidable in this age, but they are still a force to be reckoned with. We will need the combined might of the Vikes and the loyal Eirlandians, and possibly even help from the Sidheran, if they agree, to overcome them."

"I had no idea", Maeve murmured.

"Much has happened since you left," Tara answered. "You could not be two places at once, so do not upbraid yourself. You completed your mission timely and sent us information we would not have had even yet if you hadn't read parts of the Book yourself. Your mission was successful beyond our dreams and gives us a head start on the next phase."

"Now you must rest and resume your duties as First Fighdrui to the ArdRighian," said Aelfund. "You will be acting as Regent while she goes with Talisean to the Sidheran to both retrieve the Master Lifenstone and, hopefully, enlist their aid in the coming conflict."

"Regent?" repeated Maeve. "I have no skills in that regard, I am not even noble, much less royal. No one will follow me!"

"On the contrary" replied Talisean, "you are both noble and royal. You are actually a cousin to the ArdRighian on your father's side. The Old King was not the only one to have youthful dalliances with Siderhan women." He winked and smiled broadly. "I have not time now to go into your family history, but promise I will tell you all about your lineage when Tara and I return with the Lifenstone.

"Know, though, that your lineage has been told to the High Council and they have already confirmed your regency in this critical time period. Aelfund and Elaroth will be your chief advisors and you will have little real power, but it will be enough to keep the wolves of war at bay while Tara and I go a-hunting."

"It seems," said Maeve slowly, "that I am but a puppet of the fates."

"No," answered Elaroth gravely.

He stood and extended his staff of office over her. "I speak now the words of the gods, given to me in a dream but last night.

"You, Maeve of the Fighdrui, cousin of the ArdRighian, Keeper of Secrets and Lore, are not the puppet of the fates. You are the Child of Fate, and in your hands will success ultimately rest.

'When you find the Root that leads into the Darkness that Brings Light, you will become the savior of your world.' So has said the Awen, and the Awen is never mistaken."

Maeve only bowed her head in acknowledgment. Her adventures were far from over, it seemed, and her ultimate destiny was apparently fated to be the stuff of legends. "I just hope the Awen is going to cooperate," she thought to herself.

Glossary

Lifenstone—Rare, Magical-Propertied stone capable of storing messages and focusing the power of the wearer. Worn as a pentant.

Master Lifenstone—Owned and worn by ArdRighian Tara I. This stone can draw on the power of all other Lifenstones in times of great need. The Master Lifenstone will only respond to the rightful ruler or heir of Eirlandia's High Ruler; or someone of the Royal Blood that has been recognized as acting on behalf of the High Ruler.

Formorrid-A word referring to both a single member and collective of an ancient race sworn to eternal enmity with the Eirlandans and the Sidheran. They would sometimes be an ally of the Vikes in their battles with the Eirlandians.

Sidheran—Member of a race of Mages who live a mostly subterranean existence. The Sidherans are mostly neutral in the affairs of the other races, but have blood ties to Eirlandian rayalty.

Their homeland of Sidhera lies beneath the land of Eirlandia, with hidden doorways and passages throughout that land.

Drui—Magical and spiritual leaders in Eirlandian society. They are the Keepers of great ancient knowledge and power. The members are considered wise and would act as counselors to the ruling Ard-Righ or ArdRighian. The Archdrui is the leader of the Drui class.

Fighdrui—Member of a special class of Drui who are trained in warfare and spycraft, as well as lesser magics. They perform many roles in Eirlandian society including historians, storytellers (known also as bards), teachers, advisors, judges, lawyers, and special bodyguards/personal assistants to the royal family.

Vikes—Warrior race who is often at war with the Eirlandians. While not complete barbarians, their culture is not as rich and varied, since most of their energy goes to conquering territories. They sometimes ally with the Formorrid, although it is an uneasy alliance.

Skaald—Vike equivalent of a Master Drui

Wif—Vik word for a wife. Women had much less power in Vike society than in Eirlandian or Sidheran.

Righ—Petty king or tribal chieftien in Eirlandian society

Ard-Righ—High King of Eirlandia. Office is not strictly hereditary, although only certain families are eligible to be considered. The Ard Righ is voted into power by the Counsel of Righs. Once crowned the Ard-Righ usually rules until death, illness, or accident make ruling impossible.

ArdRighian-High Queen of Eirlandia. Same duties as the Ard-Righ, but female. Until Tara I there had never been an ArdRighian.

Tanist(a)—Chosen heir of ruling Ard Righ. The Tanist must be confirmed by majorty vote of the Council of Righs. Candidates must be of age and pass certain tests of both battle and general knowledge. Only certain families are allowed to put forth candidates.

Follow the further adventures of Tara and
Maeve in Book II of *Tales of Eirlandia*

About the Author

Mariclaire Norton has been interested in writing fiction since high school. She is a published poet in a Poetry Anthology, and in high school wrote and directed a play based on 'The Crucible'.

Ms. Norton has long been a fan of fantasy fiction with authors such as Anne McCaffrey, J.R.R. Tolkien and J.K. Rowlings being her inspiration and idols. She is also a long time student of Celtic and Norse mythology. Those familiar with these subjects will find some references to these cultures in her writings.

Now retired, Ms. Norton spends her time volunteering as a therapeutic music harper at a local hospital when she isn't writing or watching her three grandchildren.

CPSIA information can be obtained
at www.ICGtesting.com
Printed in the USA
JSHW060153031222
34248JS00006B/90